The
Support Group

The
Support Group

Shirley Oldridge

Oak Tree Press — Taylorville, IL

Oak Tree Press

Oak Tree Press books may be purchased for educational, business or sales promotional purposes. Contact Publisher for quantity discounts.

First Edition, July 2012

Cover by Reese-Winslow Designs
Interior Pages by Kalpart (www.kalpart.com)

ISBN 978-1-61009-105-3
LCCN 20126937976

For Nicole and Lisa

Chapter One

"And the award goes to …"

Five words that can stop time, stop breath, stop hearts. Margo squeezed Warren's hand. If nothing else, the movie had been nominated for six academy awards, and had already taken four. Warren had won best director, and the movie now boasted best picture, best original score, and best cinematography. It was an impressive collection.

It's enough to be nominated, she told herself. Whatever you do, don't look disappointed. Smile and clap, smile and clap … For God's sake, open the damn envelope!

"… Margo Priestley, for *Endangered Species*."

Finally! Margo's lungs filled with much needed air, followed by a sharp exhale. She hugged Warren tightly. "Thank you," she whispered softly into his ear. This had been the most sought-after role in Hollywood. Meryl had wanted this one, but Warren had wanted Margo.

"Congratulations, honey, you earned it. Now get up there, will ya, before they change their minds!" Warren nodded toward the stage.

The applause was thunderous, deafening. Everyone was on their feet. This was the big one: best actress in a leading role.

If only Jack had won best actor; sadly, not this year. That damn Brad Pitt! Five out of six would have to do.

The walk to the stage was a long and perilous one. She should have gone with the shorter dress, not this deathtrap that treacherously threatened to grab hold of her spiked heels. She made it up the stairs, walking calmly and confidently to the center of the stage to claim her prize. The presenter was Kelly Monroe, a svelte brunette, herself nominated for best actress in a supporting role. She should have won, Margo thought, but hey, there's always next year, and unlike Margo, youth was on her side. At least that bitch Brigitte didn't win either. That was a bonus. Margo took the award in both hands and kissed Kelly on both cheeks. She positioned herself in front of the microphone.

"Wow," she began. "Two years in a row. Look out, Meryl; I'm catching up!" In response, her good friend affectionately blew her a kiss from the audience. "First, I'd like to thank the academy for this wonderful award, and everyone who nominated and voted for me. Thank you so much. I'd like to thank my good friend, and a brilliant director, Warren Felstein, for having enough faith in me to offer me this wonderful part. Love you, Warren! I'd like to thank Jack for putting up with all my mistakes, — the swelling will go down eventually, Jack; I promise!" Laughter rose from the audience, as though everyone understood the private joke. Jack blew the customary kiss back. "I'd also like to thank all the cast and crew. You guys were amazing! This award is as much yours as mine; I'll just hold on to it for you." Again laughter rang out, a little forced, Margo thought. "And last but not least, my beautiful daughter, Cassidy. Thank you for all your love and support, and for believing in me. I wish you could be here with me tonight. I love you, baby!"

Margo proudly held her award up high, and smiling, exited stage left. Thank God that was over with! Acting was one thing, but standing in front of an audience, in addition to millions of live television viewers, scared the crap out of her.

"This way please, Miss Priestley." A young man gestured toward a wall draped with the awards ceremony logo. Another young man waited eagerly behind a large camera. "Just a couple of shots of you holding your award, if we may."

Margo obliged willingly. This was one of the best nights of her life. Now she could relax and enjoy the rest of it. She wished her daughter could have been there. Cassidy could have made it in time had she flown, but she promised to do the drive home from the east coast with her best friend, Meghan. They had finished their last year at Harvard and Meghan wanted to drive her car back. Not Cassidy, the spendthrift. She had sold hers a few days earlier to save herself the aggravation. She'd just get a new one when she returned to L.A. Over the phone she had told Margo about a cute little Lexus convertible she liked, and had asked her if perhaps she might want to go look at it with her.

"You mean pay for it, don't you?" Margo had joked.

Cassidy had crooned sweetly. "I love you, Mommy."

Cassidy would be surprised tomorrow, thought Margo, smiling to herself, when she found her graduation present waiting in the garage. It paid to have an Oscar-winning movie star for a mom.

Chapter Two

For the most part, award parties bored Margo, although she never tired of seeing stars — real stars that was. Pacino was here tonight, Crowe, Clooney, and she had just received a celebratory hug from Robert DeNiro.

She always loved spending time with Meryl, of course. One of them was always working on a project somewhere, so the few minutes they spent with each other tonight laughing were worth a small fortune. They promised faithfully to get together for lunch before being whisked in opposite directions for publicity reasons. Her feet were killing her, yet sitting down was out of the question. She was, after all, the "best actress" this year. She had obligations. There were countless photographs and autographs and interviews. The food looked great, and probably was, but in this dress she couldn't actually eat anything. Not if she didn't want to resemble a post natal wallaby in the tabloids. Especially not after all the dieting she had done during the week. She'd already had two glasses of wine, so she had better leave that alone, too. Too many paparazzi wanted to catch pictures of the stars drooling all over themselves, exposing private body parts as they exited cars, and since Margo hadn't eaten a thing, she might well end up in one of those pictures if she drank anymore. She wanted out of there, badly. She wanted her pajamas, slippers, and a cheese pizza.

Her cell phone vibrated in her purse, shattering the images of comfort in her head. Margo excused herself from the current company and slipped into the hallway. She rifled through the purse, retrieving her phone.

"Hello?" she answered. The phone crackled.

"Mom?" Cassidy's voice sounded weak. There was a lot of background noise.

"Hey, honey, where are you?" Margo was looking forward to spending time with her daughter. It had been over eight months since graduation. Cassidy and Meghan decided to spend the summer after college ended in Maine and the fall in New York with friends. They had flown to L.A. for Christmas and the New Year, but had returned to the east coast in January to retrieve their belongings from Boston. Margot had just received a shipment of boxes containing Cassidy's books and clothing. Now the girls were driving back in Meghan's '79 Mustang. They had been lucky with the weather, one of Margo's main concerns. February was a terrible month to drive across country.

"We're in Arizona, near Phoenix. We should get to San Diego by tomorrow afternoon. Meghan will drop me off at Dad's on the way to her parents' house."

"Where are you now? What's all that noise?" Margo strained to hear Cassidy.

"We're in a bar. It's a little loud in here. We just had something to eat. Now we're going to get a room."

"Call me from the hotel." Margo felt uneasy. She was extremely uncomfortable with the whole 'two girls driving across country alone' thing.

"Mom, please! We'll be fine. I'll see you tomorrow night. Dad already said he'd fly me up. I don't have a car, remember?"

"Is he expecting you? Make sure he knows that you're coming."

"I will, Mom. Don't worry, I have a key. By the way, I caught the awards on the news. Congratulations, Mom! I'm so proud of you. I love you!"

"I love you too, baby! Call me when you get to your dad's."

"Okay, Mom; love you. Bye!"

"Bye, baby!"

Chapter Three

Margo sipped her coffee and thumbed through the morning paper. Three more gang-related deaths. What a terrible waste. A woman was raped while walking on the beach at three in the morning. *What the hell was she doing on the beach at three in the morning?* Margo wondered. She tried not to be so judgmental. *You should be safe to walk the beach whenever the hell you want,* she justified. A two-year-old was savagely mauled by a pit bull. His father had left the child alone in the apartment with the dog while he stood outside talking to a neighbor. "They should throw him in with a bunch of pit bulls!" she said aloud.

"Throw who in with a bunch of pit bulls?" her housekeeper, Carla, asked from across the kitchen.

"This asshole!" Margo answered vehemently, tapping the paper with her index finger. "I swear. I'd love to slap the crap out of some of these people! You have to take a test to finish school, to get a job, to drive a car, but any idiot is allowed to be a parent. You should have to take an IQ test, and if you fail, snip-snip, knot-knot. That would remedy the situation."

"Wow! I'm glad you're not president! My son-in-law would never pass. I'd never be a grandmother." Carla had been around since the early days of Margo's pregnancy. Jim had hired Carla not totally convinced that Margo would be the most capable mother in the world. Margo had actually surprised everyone with how good she was in the role, which gave Carla quite a bit of free time in the beginning, until Margo was finally convinced that she had proven herself to the rest of the family. Then she relinquished the mommy reins to Carla — somewhat — without ever actually stepping aside.

Margo was a good boss. Carla's son and daughter had both moved up to the Bay Area with their families. When Carla's husband passed away last fall from cancer, Margo had generously offered to give Carla the beach house. Jim had been moved out for almost a year now, so it was about time that someone put his 'man cave' to good use. It was a completely self-sufficient two-bedroom property, with a three-car garage, an ocean view, and beach access. Margo had called it Jim's, but had originally built it to house Sylvia, Jim's mother, when she visited. That woman had more ailments than Carters had pills. She couldn't stay in one of the many upstairs bedrooms because of the stairs. She couldn't stay in the downstairs back suite because it was too close to the laundry facilities; the detergent aggravated her allergies. That left Cassidy's room and the downstairs master suite, and Margo had absolutely no intention of giving up either. So the 'man cave' was built on the property. Sylvia complained that it was too far away from the house. Margo thought it was too close. Sadly, she only stayed in it three times before passing away quietly in her sleep in the comfort of her own home.

Margo had it redecorated in rich woods and dark leathers to appeal to Jim's masculine side. She must have infused too much testosterone, though, because less than six months after its completion, she arrived home early to find Jim christening the bear skin in what was now his study, with Brigitte Cavelle, his latest leading lady. In his defense, Jim had complained that Margo's three-month absence, while working on *Last Summer in Seville*, had pushed him into Brigitte's arms. Bullshit! Margo had had many chances to play catcher to jumping directors; she had simply chosen not to. So, as a result, Jim left to become Brigitte's boytoy in San Diego, Cassidy was away at Harvard, and Margo was alone in this mausoleum. It had made perfect sense to turn Jim's 'man cave' into Carla's rent-free, beach front property. It helped Carla out financially, saving her from moving in with her daughter and the idiot husband in San Francisco, and Margo now had company. She hated to be alone.

"That fucking bitch!" Margot spat. "Where's the phone?" She rose suddenly and headed for the kitchen counter, her outstretched arm reaching for the cordless phone cradled on the wall ahead of her.

Carla quickly perused the open newspaper, searching for the offensive article that had caused the outburst. "Hollywood Director to Wed French Star!" the headline read. There was a five-by-seven picture of Jim and Brigitte locked in a lovers' embrace, Brigitte smiling overly large-mouthed, perfectly posed for the paparazzi. "There will be a marriage before the end of the year, sources claim.

Brigitte has been heard talking about a Christmas wedding," Carla read aloud.

"Sources claim, my ass! She did this on purpose. She purposely leaked this now to overshadow the awards ceremony." Margo punched the numbers on the keypad. "Pick up, asshole," she said through clenched teeth.

"Hello." Jim's voice sounded meek. Caller ID was a wonderful warning system. "Margo, don't go off half-cocked. I don't know where they got that. I haven't even asked Brigitte to marry me."

"You don't know?" Margo asked sarcastically. "I'll tell you where they got it. That frog bitch, that's where they got it!

"That's enough name-calling, Margo," Jim stated calmly.

"Enough?" Margo huffed. "If I were to call her a two-faced lying slut and a home-wrecking whore it still wouldn't be enough!!"

"Margo! There's no need for this!" Jim's voice pleaded with her.

"Is this how you tell your daughter that you're getting married?" Margo continued feverishly. "And why at Christmas, Jim? Is it because you and Cassidy always spend Christmas in Aspen? She's slowly but surely erasing every part of your life, pre-Brigitte."

"That will never happen," Jim answered adamantly. "No one makes decisions for me. If and when I decide to get married again, you and Cassidy will be the first to know."

"Just make sure you let Cassidy know. I personally couldn't give a rat's ass!" Margo hit the talk button. She was shaking as she replaced it on the wall loudly. She retook her seat, leaning back in the chair. Running her fingers through her hair, she cradled the back of her head in her hands.

"Feel better now?" Carla asked sarcastically. Margo didn't answer.

The phone rang suddenly, causing both women to jump. "If it's that asshole …" Margo growled. Carla grabbed the phone before she could do more damage.

"Hello," she said. "Oh. Hi, Jerri! Yes, she's right here." She held the receiver out to Margo. "It's Jerri," she repeated unnecessarily.

"Hi, hon!" The voice on the other end of the phone chirped. Jerri Maddox had been Margo's friend and confidant since high school. "Congratulations!" she warbled. "I would have called you last night, but I couldn't stay up that late."

"Thank you, darling. Are we still on for lunch on Tuesday?"

"Absolutely!" Her friend paused. "Did you read the paper today?" she asked gingerly.

"Yeessss!" Margo hissed. "I already spoke to Jim about it."

"Spoke?" Carla raised her eyebrows.

"We all know who's responsible for that." Margot continued, ignoring Carla. "I'm not going to let it get to me."

"Yeah, right!" Carla muttered leaving the room.

"Listen. Have you spoken to the girls today?" Jerri sounded concerned.

"Cassi called me last night." Margo replied.

"Yeah, Meg called me, too. She said she was going to call me this morning. I've called her cell, but it goes straight to voicemail." Jerri always was a worrier, and way overprotective. Margo had been surprised to hear that she had agreed to let Meghan drive back at all, even if Cassidy was with her. She thought back to the time they both took the "Mommy and Me" swimming classes. The instructor had told them to plunge their babies under the water quickly, laughing and cooing as they re-emerged into the air. Jerri had been unable to push her six-month-old daughter underwater. Margo had teased her relentlessly.

"Maybe they're out of range," Margo offered. "Cassi said they should be at Jim's this afternoon. I forgot to ask if he'd heard from her."

"Will you call me if you hear from them? I'm getting a little worried. It's not like Meg; she always calls when she says she will." Jerri sighed heavily.

"As soon as I speak to Cassi I'll call you. Meghan will probably call you first, though." Margo didn't know why, but she felt uneasy. Her stomach suddenly felt queasy.

"Morg. Would you …? Could you check to see if Jim has heard from them yet?" Jerri urged. "I'd feel a lot better."

"Yeah, sure," Margo answered hesitantly. "Shit," she thought. "Now I have to call Jim back."

Chapter Four

Margo threw the Frisbee almost the full length of the beach. Annie raced after it. Margo wished she had a quarter of the energy that dog had. She reached into her jacket pocket and pulled out her cell phone, checking to see if perhaps she had missed a call from Cassidy. Nothing. She was supposed to have called when she hit Jim's. Margo had already called Cassi's phone a few times, but it had gone straight to voice mail. *It must be turned off,* she thought. She dialed Jim's home number, again. It rang twice, then went to the answering machine, which told Margo he hadn't even listened to the messages she had left for him earlier. Where the hell was he? He was supposed to have been here last night, with Cassidy. He hadn't answered his phone since their argument yesterday morning, which was hardly surprising. She didn't have his new cell phone number. He had called her from his cell a few times, but apparently, she hadn't saved the number.

She looked at her watch again … two thirty-five. What if they had been in an accident on the way up? Her stomach churned. She pondered calling the police to see if anything had been reported, involving either car or plane. No, she shook her head to destroy the very idea. She probably wouldn't feel as anxious if it wasn't for Jerri calling every two hours to find out if she'd heard anything. Maybe she should try Cassidy again. She scrolled through her call log to Cassidy's number, selected it, and hit the dial button.

"Hello!" said the familiar voice.

"Cassidy Marsden, where the hell …"

"I'm sorry, but I'm unavailable right now," the familiar voice interrupted. "I promise I'll get back to you …"

Margo snapped the phone closed. Now she was mad. This was the most irresponsible thing Cassidy had ever done. Well, maybe she wouldn't be getting that car after all. It was funny how Cassidy always answered her friends' calls. Those stupid text messages, too.

Text messages! Margo typed as quickly as a woman who never texts can.

CASSIDY WHERE ARE YOU MOM. She didn't know how to make the period or question mark; it would have to do. She hit the send button.

"Margo!"

Margo looked up at the patio. There was Jim, waving frantically. She breathed a loud sigh; thank God! She called to the dog and hastened up the beach to the stairs leading to the patio. She scaled them two at a time, anxious to see her little girl. She was winded when she reached the top.

"Jesus Christ!" she exclaimed. "Can't you people answer your phones? I've been worried sick here, imagining all kinds of ..."

Jim's face was serious, too serious. Margo looked around. "What? Where's Cassidy?"

"Morg, we need to fly to Phoenix. The police called ..."

"What happened? Were they in an accident? Are they okay?" Margo fired the questions at him.

"They found Meghan's car just outside Phoenix. They don't know where Meghan is yet. They think they have Cassi." He hung his head.

"They think they have Cassi?" she echoed. "What do you mean, they think they have Cassi?"

"They want us to make," he paused, "a positive ID."

Margo didn't know how she got there, but suddenly, she was on her knees. Her hands were stinging from the sudden impact with the floor. Her chest felt as though it were about to explode from her heart beating hard against her ribs. Her legs were gone; she couldn't feel them. And what the hell was that noise? Suddenly, she recognized the sound — her own uncontrollable screaming.

Chapter Five

The walls of the Maricopa County Medical Examiner's office were painted a stark white. It reminded Margo of a hospital, only nobody was going to be miraculously cured here. There were no expectant fathers running in, flowers in hand. No seven-year-old budding gold medalists sporting pink arm casts. No frantic mothers, awaiting the results of their eleven-year-olds' emergency appendectomies. No visitors, no patients, just dead people; a big building, full of dead people. And one of them might be Cassidy. Margo shook her head. Get that thought out of there. It wasn't Cassidy … It wasn't Cassidy.

The flight from L.A. had taken only an hour in the small private jet. Normally, Jim allowed no-one to fly his plane, but he didn't trust his judgment today. He had hired one of the freelance pilots who worked out of the private airport to take them to Phoenix and back. Margo couldn't recall one word spoken between them the whole flight. In fact the only words she remembered hearing at all were when Jim had exchanged a token greeting with the limo driver at the Phoenix airport waiting to take them directly to the morgue. Halfway through the car trip she had been surprised to realize that she had been holding Jim's hand, tightly. Their eyes had met momentarily, and he had squeezed her fingers tenderly. No words were necessary.

When they arrived, they were ushered into a waiting area, where they sat anxiously. A door to their left opened, and a small-framed man in a lab coat with a bald head and glasses emerged. "Mr. and Mrs. Marsden?" he nodded toward them. He pushed his glasses up the bridge of his nose.

"Yes," Jim said quickly. They both stood.

"I'm Dr. Lewis; we spoke on the phone." He shook Jim's hand. He pushed his glasses up the bridge of his nose again. His voice sounded nervous, anxious. "We actually only need one of you for the identification. Mrs. Marsden, my assistant Helen will wait here with you." A young red-haired girl stepped from behind Dr. Lewis.

"Hello, Mrs. Marsden. Can I get you something to drink? A tea or coffee perhaps?"

"No, I don't want something to drink!" Margo snapped. "I want to see if you have my daughter in there!"

"I think it might be best if just one of you were to come with me right now." Dr. Lewis looked directly into Jim's eyes. "Just for a few moments," he added. Jim nodded.

"Oh, my God! Oh, my God! Why don't you want me to see her? What the hell happened to her?" Margo was visibly shaking. Helen helped her into the chair behind her. She buried her head in her hands, her shaking shoulders, the only indication that she was crying. Helen quietly took Jim's place in the chair beside her, while he silently vanished through the door with Dr. Lewis.

A million thoughts raced through Margo's head. She knew it wasn't a car accident. The police had found Meghan's car abandoned. That much she knew. But nobody knew where Meghan was. That didn't make sense. Cassidy and Meghan had been joined at the hip since infancy. Margo had been thrilled when her best friend had declared she also was pregnant, just two weeks after Margo had announced her own news to the media. Jerri and Margo had gone to prenatal classes together. Cassidy arrived a week late, while Meghan was two weeks early, leaving only eleven days between their birthdays. They had learned to swim together, horseback ride together, cheerlead together. They talked every day of their lives. Meghan would never leave Cassidy alone in Phoenix. No, Cassidy had to be somewhere else with Meghan. Safe. Whoever they had in that room, it wasn't Cassidy. It was just some other girl with long dark brown hair. Some other girl found alone in a wooded area, fifteen miles from the hotel. She must have stolen Cassidy's purse. Was it even Cassidy's purse? There was no wallet inside. No cell phone. Just a library card. Just Cassidy Marsden's Harvard student library card. But it wasn't Cassidy. It wasn't Cassidy.

Jim emerged through the door. His face was ashen, expressionless. He stood silently, staring. Margo thought he swayed a little, unsteady on his feet. His eyes closed slowly. He nodded. Margo rose.

"No," she whimpered. "It can't be her. It can't be." Her breathing grew erratic. "I … I want to see her! I want to see my baby!" She moved toward the door.

Jim's left hand shot out to secure the door, his right hand firmly held in front of Margo's chest. "You can't go in there!" he was adamant.

"Oh, my God, Jim!" she gasped. "What did they do to her?"

Without warning, Jim turned suddenly and vomited violently.

Margo screamed, "What the hell did they do to her?!"

Chapter Six

"The search for twenty-three-year-old Meghan Maddox ended shortly after seven pm last night, when her body was discovered by teenagers in a Yuma, Arizona skate park. The body of her best friend, Cassidy Marsden, daughter of actress Margo Preistley and director Jim Marsden, was found four days earlier in a wooded area outside Phoenix. The two went missing late Sunday night, their abandoned car was discovered in the parking lot of a Phoenix restaurant, early Monday morning. Police have not yet released the cause of death of either girl, but have declared both cases to be homicide. It is not known yet whether the murders were sexually motivated, or if the crimes took place at the sites where the bodies were discovered. At this time the police have no suspects or persons of interest and are asking that anyone with any knowledge in either case, please contact them at the number on the screen. A private ceremony for the family and close friends of Cassidy Marsden was held today in an undisclosed location. The families of the two girls ask that their privacy be respected at this time….. More on the Anaheim liquor store robberies …"

Jim pointed the remote at the TV; it fell silent. *How the hell did it come to this?* Frank Maddox had called around eleven the night before to excuse himself and Jerri from attending Cassidy's funeral. They had to fly to Yuma. Jim had almost cried, knowing the kind of vision that awaited them. What the hell do you say to someone to comfort them, when you already know what kind of monster has their daughter? As soon as Jim had returned from Phoenix Frank called, demanding to know what had happened to Cassidy. Jim pretty much knew that the same fate was in store for Meghan, if it hadn't already taken place. At Frank's insistence, he had finally told him that Cassidy had died from asphyxiation, and yes, she had been sexually assaulted, but had refused to say anything more. Frank didn't need to know the gruesome details, nor did Margo. Jim sobbed, and then quickly stifled his sorrow. He was a good man, perhaps not the best father or husband in the world, but a good man nonetheless. An easygoing, laid-back kind of guy. Yet right now he felt as though he wanted to kill someone, anyone. He wanted to beat someone to death with his bare hands. He wanted to find the bastard who had killed his little girl, and choke him to death by cramming his own underwear down his throat.

The vibrating of his cell phone startled him. He quickly retrieved it from his jacket pocket. He checked the number. "Brigitte?"

"Where are you? Are you still at Margo's?" Her heavy French accent sounded agitated.

"Yes. I told you I would be here all night." He rubbed his eyes and pinched the bridge of his nose.

"I don't see why you 'ave to stay there. She 'as an 'ousekeeper." There was definitely no love lost between Brigitte and Margo.

"I'm not leaving her tonight. I told you this." He was getting irritated. "We need to be here for each other right now."

"So you just push me aside? I'm 'ere for you. What about me?"

"I'll be home tomorrow." He was growing tired of the conversation.

"Did you tell 'er?"

"Tell her what?"

"You know what!" Brigitte was getting annoyed. "France! Did you tell 'er we're moving to France?"

"That's not definite! We only discussed that as a possibility. Jesus, Brigitte!" Sometimes he wanted to scream.

"You said that you couldn't move because of Cassidy. Well! Now you can." She was so matter-of-fact, it was unbelievable.

"I'm hanging up now," Jim said through a clenched jaw. "I'm going to turn off my phone. Don't try to call me here." True to his word he hung up and turned off the phone immediately. He placed it back in his pocket. He shook his head in disbelief. She was probably the most beautiful woman he had ever met, but God, was she ugly on the inside.

Carla walked out of Margo's room. "She doesn't want to take the pills." She nodded toward the door. "Maybe she'll listen to you."

Jim took a deep breath and opened the door. Margo was sitting on the side of the bed staring through the oceanfront window, which at this time of night, reflected back like a huge black mirror. She stared up at him. *He always looked good in black,* she thought. He was a handsome man, always had been. She remembered the first time she saw him. He had worn those jeans well, very well. Margo had a thing for athletic bodies. You could have the sexiest eyes in the world, but if the chest and the butt didn't match, no way. She smiled. The gut was expanding a little. All that French cooking. Little Miss Ooh La Lah was only twenty-eight. She could afford to eat like that. An hour a day in the gym kept her a trim size two. Jim on the other hand was forty-five, and couldn't spell gym, unless it was his name on a check. His black hair was graying at the temples. Did that just happen? He had a beautiful face, much better-looking than her own, she thought. He should have gone into acting, too; he had the look.

He had been studying cinematography in college, while she was a drama geek. Jerri had noticed him first. Jerri had a hell of a body in college. She had a rack to die for. If she had had a clearer complexion Jim might have asked her out, instead of Margo. Thank god for acne! She was Morgan Ryder then, but had picked out the name of Margo Preistley when she was twelve-years-old. She knew she was going to be a star. She practiced writing her autograph on everything she owned. She handed a copy to Jim in the cafeteria with her number on the bottom. "Hang on to this," she told him. "When you shoot your first movie, call me." He actually called her that night, and he did put her in his first movie.

"You need to take those pills. You look like shit, Morg." He sat down beside her.

"I will," she muttered. "I just don't want to sleep right now." Her eyes drifted to the dressing table. The light was blinking on her cell phone. "I have a message."

"Check it in the morning. Right now you need to sleep." Jim rose to fetch the glass of water and pills from her bedside table. As he did Margo got up and walked to the dresser. She flipped open her phone.

"Oh, my God! It's from Cassi!" she shrieked.

Someone had replied to Margo's text message, the words all in capital letters:

IM DEAD MOM
AND SO IS MEGHAN IN ABOUT TEN MINUTES
BYE

Margo trembled as she clicked on the attachment that had been sent with the text message. There was a naked Meghan, ankles bound and gagged. A young man was behind her, obviously tying her hands behind her back. Jim slowly took the phone from Margo's shaking hand. He placed it carefully on the dresser, so as not to accidentally delete anything. He sat Margo back down on the bed.

"Carla!" he yelled. "Call the police!"

Chapter Seven

Margo brushed her hair toward the nape of her neck and secured it with a clip. She stared at her reflection. *Who the hell was that?* She had aged twenty years, she thought. She had always been told that she had the sexiest blue eyes, but today they were a dull gray. She looked in disbelief at her sallow complexion, the dark shadows, lost weight evident in her gaunt face. It was definitely not the face of an Oscar winning film star. Sadly, she no longer cared. She couldn't actually remember eating recently. She must have, she thought, the way Jim and Carla were hovering over her all the time. *Eat something, Margo. Have something to drink, Margo. Why don't you lie down, Margo? Did you take your pills?* She wished they would just leave her alone. Her bathroom had become her favorite place in the house, a safe haven, a sanctuary. It had a lock on the door.

"Margo?" Jim tapped on the bathroom door. Margo cringed. What the hell was it now? "Margo, there's a Detective Sawyer here. He wants to speak to us both."

"I'll be right out." She sighed heavily, then picked up her lipstick tube and removed the top. Who was she kidding? She threw both pieces onto the dressing table and stood up. She addressed herself in the mirror. "Let's go hear some more good news."

"Here she is." Jim gestured toward Margo as she emerged through the bedroom door. "Margo, this is Detective Sawyer." Margo nodded.

"Hello, Ms. Priestley," Sawyer began. "I'm sorry we have to meet under such …"

"Yeah. Whatever." Margo waved him off. "Did you find him yet?" She took a seat on the arm of an overstuffed chair. Jim shook his head in disbelief. Margo was never rude to anyone. Well, anyone but Brigitte. She must really be hurting.

"Not yet, Ms. Priestley. But we will." He pointed to the sofa. "May I sit down?" Margo nodded. "We traced a message sent from Cassidy's phone. It was picked up by a tower five miles from the place shown in the photograph you received. When we swept the area we did in fact find that site; however, that's not where we found Meghan's body. We actually found the body of the young man in the photograph. At the time, we didn't know the two were connected, now after seeing that photograph, we do."

"Who was he? Do you have a name?" Margo leaned forward in her seat.

"No, he had nothing on him that would give us any clues as to his identity. Whoever killed him took Meghan, and killed her a couple of hours later. We don't know if this young man knew the killer or was just another victim found along the way."

"So this guy didn't kill her right after the phone call, like he said?" Jim shook his head. "Why send that message, and then not do it?"

"For God's sake, Jim!" Margo interrupted. "This is a murderer we're talking about. You want to know why he lied. Does it matter?"

"It might, Ms. Priestley," Sawyer interrupted. "Something may have happened to stop him from carrying out his original plan. The young man in the picture may have had something to do with it." Sawyer replaced his pen in his handkerchief pocket. "As we uncover more evidence we'll keep you posted. Obviously, I won't be able to disclose everything."

"We understand," Jim said, sullenly. "Thank you for stopping by. We appreciate it." Jim walked toward the front door with Detective Sawyer. Margo flopped back into the armchair and closed her eyes. She could hear Jim and Sawyer talking softly in the hallway. Jim was probably excusing Margo's bad manners, she thought. He was still her greatest PR man. The telephone rang.

"Hello?" Margo answered meekly. There was no caller ID in the den.

"Allo? Margo?"

"What the hell do you want?" Margo snapped. "I told you never to call my home again."

"Where is Jim. 'E's not answering 'is phone." Brigitte sounded impatient.

"I'll tell him to call you. Don't worry, Brigitte, You'll get him back." Margo was about to hang up.

"Did 'e tell you about France?"

"What about France?"

"We are going to live there. 'E didn't tell you?"

Margo replaced the phone in the cradle. *Things just keep getting better and better,* she thought.

Chapter Eight

"Is there enough light out here?" Jim said leaning toward the camcorder.

"Yes, I think so," Carla replied.

"Great! Let's get started." Jim cleared his throat. "Ladies and gentlemen," he began. "Here to perform her new hit record, 'On White Horses,' Cassidy Marsden!" Jim did his best cheering and wolf whistling as a six-year-old Cassi appeared from behind the patio door, followed by Margo wielding an acoustic guitar. Margo took a seat on the wicker sofa behind Cassi as she centered herself in front of the camera. She began to sing, while Margo played along.

"On white horses let me ride away, to my world of dreams so far away.

Let me run, to the sun, to a world my heart can understand.

It's a warm and gentle wonderland.

Far away. Stars away.

Where the clouds are made of candy floss as the day is born.

When the stars are gone, we'll race to meet the dawn.

So when I can only see the grey of a sad and very lonely day.

That's when I softly sigh.

On white horses, snowy white horses, let me ride away."

Margo and Carla cheered and applauded wildly as Cassi bowed proudly. Jim, on the other hand, rubbed his chin and shook his head in disapproval. "I don't know, Cassi, if that was your best. Remember our deal, the better the song, the better the present."

Margo stood up defiantly. "Are you nuts? That was brilliant!"

"It could have been better." Jim was adamant.

"That was a twenty-four carat song," Margo shouted in defense of her daughter's singing debut.

"Well," said Jim. "I'll give you two carats. That's fair."

"No way!" Margo protested. "We want at least three carats!"

"I don't want carrots," Cassi said solemnly.

"Of course you do, honey," Margo corrected her. "They're for your birthday present."

"I don't like carrots!" Cassi's bottom lip was starting to quiver. "I don't want carrots!"

"They're for your birthday present, baby," Jim cooed. "Here you go." He conveniently pulled three carrots from his back jeans pocket, and held them out for Cassi to take.

"I don't want carrots!" Cassi stamped her foot.

" No, but your birthday present does," Margo said, gently turning Cassi's face in the direction of the beach. There stood Mark, Margo's brother, holding the reins of a beautiful white pony. Cassi squealed with pleasure and started for the stairs to the beach.

"Hey, wait a minute. Are you forgetting something?" Jim called.

Cassi spun around, raced back, and grabbed the carrots from Jim's hand. Once again she headed for the beach.

"I was kind of hoping for a kiss, or a hug," Jim complained.

"Awww! Come here, Daddy!" Margo slipped her arms around Jim's waist and kissed him affectionately on the lips.

"Excuse me," said a voice from behind the camera. "I'm still filming here," Carla reminded them.

"Well, in that case," said Jim, and he pulled Margo backward and began to kiss her passionately.

Margo smiled to herself as her eyes slowly closed. The home movies brought back memories that danced in her head. Cassi had whined so much about not being able to wear a pretty dress to sing for daddy. Margot had insisted she wear the stirrup pants and a long sleeve t-shirt. Of course Cassi didn't know about the pony on the beach, so she couldn't understand why her mom didn't want to put her hair up in a pretty little chignon, with curls cascading at either side of her adorable little face. Instead, Margo had opted to put Cassi's hair in two pigtails. Chignons and riding helmets don't go together. Cassi had been anything but pleased with her mother prior to the performance.

Margo's mind drifted. Now she was standing on the beach. She felt peaceful, calm, sedate. Her eye caught a glimpse of something a little way down the beach. Gradually the vision became clearer as it drew closer. A beautiful young woman on a white horse was galloping toward her. In her hand she held the reins of a second white horse that ran beside her. As she drew nearer, Margo smiled in recognition.

"Mom!" The vision called, shaking her head to flick her long dark hair out of her face. She was smiling warmly. "I have one here for you. Get on. Come with me."

Margo started to walk toward the horse.

"Margo!" Jim's voice called from the deck.

"Come on, Mom!" Cassi called playfully.

"I'm coming, baby!" Margo called back to Cassi, ignoring Jim."

"Margo! Come back!" Jim sounded impatient. Margo continued walking. She held out her hands for the reins. "Margo! Stay with me, Margo!" God, Jim was annoying. Margo suddenly felt a stinging sensation on the left side of her face. What the hell was that? She turned to look at Jim. He was blurry now, out of focus. He seemed so far away. She shook her head and peered in his direction. Everything was growing dark. She heard a ripping sound.

"Margo, open your eyes!" Again came the stinging sensation, this time on the right. What the hell was that? It was dark now, and warm. Margo could feel herself melting into the darkness. It was peaceful there in the dark.

Jim frantically wrapped the torn sheets around the gaping slashes on Margo's wrists. He had never seen this much blood before. At least not off the movie set anyway.

"The ambulance is on the way!" Carla shouted. "I'll wait outside for them."

"Margo!" He bellowed, slapping her again. "Open your fucking eyes!"

Chapter Nine

Margo's eyes flickered open. The room was bright, way too bright. She closed them again. Her second attempt proved more successful. Her surroundings were blurry, but she could tell immediately that they were unfamiliar. A low continuous beeping noise was coming from somewhere. The air smelled strange. There was a light scent of disinfectant, although not the floral kind she liked. She swallowed. It hurt, bad. She would make a point of not swallowing again if she could help it, she thought. But as is always the case with bodily functions, when you try not to, you do them nonstop. She tried to put her hand to her throat. Something was holding both her arms down. She tried to lift her head to see what was restricting her arms; she couldn't. She was too weak.

"So, you finally decided to wake up!" Jim's voice came from her right.

She rolled her head to one side to look in his direction. She could see his blurred outline standing in what appeared to be a doorway. She blinked. Slowly everything began to come into focus. He was leaning against the door frame, his arms folded. She swallowed again, and groaned audibly.

"Sore throat?" He approached the bed. "Must be that vacuum cleaner hose they had to stick down there." He stood towering over her. The expression on his face was anything but pleasant. "Little overkill, don't you think Margo? Sleeping pills and wrist slashing."

She didn't answer. She knew there was nothing she could say in her defense. Had it worked, she wouldn't have had to say anything. Jim continued relentlessly. "You kind of saved yourself though, honey," he said sarcastically. "Those sleeping pills slowed your heartbeat down so much, you didn't get to pump it all out fast enough, and we found you in time."

"What are you doing here?" she asked in a hoarse whisper. "I thought you left."

"If you remember, I flew commercial. My flight was delayed due to fog. Good thing, really, 'cause that's when Carla called to tell me that you had locked all the doors and you wouldn't answer your phone."

"She was supposed to have left for San Francisco," Margo sighed, eyes closed.

"Foiled again, Moriarty!" Jim said without attempting to disguise his sarcasm. "I just told you, it was foggy out. She had to turn back. She saw all your lights on and heard the television. She knew you weren't asleep. You never sleep. When she realized you had double-bolted every door, she called me. By the way, you need a new patio door." He sat down on the edge of the bed.

"You broke the patio door?" Secretly, she was impressed.

"Well, I couldn't smash through the wooden one," he offered in his defense.

"I can't move my arms," she complained.

"That's because you attempted suicide. They want to make sure you're not going to try anything stupid again before they unfasten those straps. Besides, they don't want you to move your wrists. You really did a number on them." He sighed heavily and rubbed his eyes. They were red. "What the hell were you thinking? Did you even think about how this would affect anyone else?" He sighed again. "What about me Margo? I just lost my daughter! What was I supposed to do when you died?" He looked away quickly, but not in time to conceal the tears that had filled his eyes.

"I just wanted it to stop hurting," she murmured in her defense. A tear ran down her cheek. "I don't want to hurt anymore." Jim held her hand in response. He gently wiped the tear away with the back of his free hand. The two sat quietly, neither really knowing what else to say.

Someone coughed in the doorway. It was the kind of cough that said, "*I know this is awkward, but I'm coming in anyway.*" Jim stood up and offered his hand to the man in the white coat.

"Hello, Doctor," he said, shaking his hand. "As you can see, she finally woke up."

"Ms. Priestley. Glad to see you're awake. I'm Doctor Morris. How are you feeling?" He approached the bed.

"I feel like shit," she retorted. "My throat hurts, I have pain in my lower back, and I can't sit up. This wasn't what I had planned."

"Well," he began, "I think you know why your throat hurts, so I'll spare you the details. Your back pain is probably due to the beating you gave your kidneys last night. Judging by the results of the blood tests, you didn't do too much damage to them, or the liver, but you did give them a workout. They'll hurt for a while. As for the straps, I'm afraid the hospital psychologist will have to make the call on whether or not he thinks you are a hazard to yourself. He'll be by in about an hour."

"When can I get out of here?" she asked. "I'd rather be miserable at home."

"Like I said, the psychologist will be here in an hour or so. He's the one who will make that decision. You'll probably have to agree to see a therapist either here, or one of your own choosing." Dr. Morris wrote something on Margo's chart.

"A shrink? I'm not talking to a shrink!" Margo raised her eyebrows defiantly.

"I'm pretty sure you'll be expected to agree to attend some kind of therapy or counseling before the hospital will release you." Dr. Morris raised his shoulders. "You'll most probably be advised to join a support group."

"A support group?!" Margo croaked.

"Yes. For the families of victims of violent …"

"I know what the hell a support group is!" Margo shouted gravelly. "I'm not joining any damn support group!!"

Chapter Ten

"Hello. My name's Doug Ryan."

"Hello, Doug," the group chimed.

"I'm the chief fire marshal for Los Angeles County." The tall sandy-haired man stared at his hands while he spoke.

"We only use first names here Doug, and you don't have to give out any private information," said the heavy-set blonde lady, smiling broadly.

"Oh, okay. I moved out here three years ago after my dad died. My parents had moved out here when my father retired from the NYPD in ninety-eight. He was born in L.A. and most of his family, or what was left of them, were still out here. My mother only had a brother in the Bronx, and me in Long Island, so she agreed to the move." He shrugged his shoulders. "Within two years, both my father's sisters had passed away, and his brother was put into a care facility because of Alzheimer's. When my dad died my mother was left out here alone. So I applied for the position of chief fire marshal out here and relocated. I've been a fire fighter for thirty-two years," he said, as if justifying his job placement. "About three months ago, while I was at work, someone broke into the apartment." Doug paused, still staring at his hands. He took a deep breath, exhaled loudly, and again began recounting his story. "The guy was on meth. He sexually assaulted my seventy-three-year-old mother and then beat her to death with a bat." He closed his eyes and pinched the bridge of his nose with his hand as if he were trying to stop a flow of emotion. He continued, "I haven't been dealing with it very well. They told me that if I didn't want to take a mandatory leave of absence, I had to come here twice a week. I've already taken as much time off as I can afford. So here I am."

"Did they catch him?" An attractive older black woman asked.

"Yes," he replied. "But that doesn't make me feel any better. Now if I could beat him to death with my bare hands — that would make me feel better." He clenched his big fists leaving no doubt in anyone's mind that he could do it.

"They're getting ready to release the man who killed my daughter," said the black woman.

"Name, dear," the heavy-set blonde lady prompted.

"Oh, I'm sorry," she corrected herself. "My name's Georgia."

"Hello, Georgia," the group chimed. Georgia rolled her eyes.

"He sold crack to my daughter until she became an addict. She lost everything. She went from being a successful realtor to being out on the street with her nine-year-old-daughter." She sat up proud in her chair.

"She OD'd on crack?" Doug guessed.

"No. She was murdered." She looked angry. "The man who killed her set his pit bulls on her — three of them. He claimed she was on his property and the dogs were justified in attacking her. They tore her to pieces. They conveniently ran away after. He was given two years for manslaughter."

"How do you know he set the dogs on her?" A Hispanic man in his mid-twenties asked.

"He told me he did." She bit her bottom lip. "I tried to help my daughter. At one time I had them both living with me. Things started to go missing from the apartment. I knew she was selling them for drug money, but she would never admit it to me. In the end I had to tell her to leave. She left her daughter with me, which I was really happy about. I didn't want Monique around the people her mother was associating with. One day, when I went to pick her up from school, she wasn't there. The teacher told me her mother had picked her up early. I walked the streets for three hours looking for them. When I got back Monique was sitting outside my door crying. She told me that her mama had taken her to a man and told her to do whatever the man wanted. When my daughter had nothing left to sell, she had traded her child. She sold my granddaughter for crack."

"Oh, my God!" said a younger black woman with afro hair.

"My daughter returned to the apartment the next day. I refused to open the door. I told her what Monique said had happened and I had reported it to the police. She said something about Monique didn't belong to her anymore. I didn't really know what she meant by that. She ran off, and that was the last time I saw my daughter alive … through the spy hole in my apartment door. The police came to tell me she was dead the next morning." She paused and closed her eyes. "About a month ago two young men came to my apartment. They said that my daughter had made a deal with Mr. Moon. She hadn't kept her end of the bargain, and so Mr. Moon had had to make an example of her. She was supposed to leave Monique with him, but Monique had gotten away from him and run to my place. Monique now belonged to Mr. Moon, and he had the right to do whatever he wanted with her. They told me that if I can come up with twenty-five thousand dollars by next month, when Mr. Moon gets out of jail, I can keep my grandbaby. If not, I have to give her up to them. If I go to the police Mr. Moon will kill us both. They said we are being watched, so don't even try to run." Georgia hung her head, a look of desolation on her face.

"That's bullshit, man!" said the young Hispanic man. "I work at the state penitentiary in Lancaster. The inmates there will rip child abusers apart. Is that this guy's real name?" He leaned forward in his seat, clearly agitated by the story he had just heard.

"That's his street name. His real name is Delroy Haines."

"I guess being named after boxers ain't scary enough!" the younger black woman said.

"Man! If he was being held where I work, I'd put his name out there and get his ass kicked daily!" The young Hispanic man was using a lot of wild hand gestures.

"That's not the way." A prim-looking Hispanic woman spoke up. "Violence only brings more violence. The justice system will deal with him."

"Lady, you on crack?" the younger black woman asked. "The justice system don't do shit!"

"You're wrong! The man who killed my husband was just sentenced to life in prison." The Hispanic lady seemed almost proud. "He's off the streets. He won't be car-jacking anyone else. He can't hurt anyone anymore."

"I disagree, honey," Georgia interjected. "His actions are going to hurt you every day, for the rest of your life."

"But that's why we're here! We have each other to share our grief with." The Hispanic lady looked around the group in earnest. "Remember? 'Sharing is healing!' We have to share and then forgive. Only then can we heal."

"Uh huh?" said the younger black woman. "Someone needs to tell that to *her*." She nodded in Margo's direction. "She ain't shared shit all the time she's been coming here."

Margo raised one eyebrow, glared at the younger black lady, and opened her mouth to speak. Then, thinking better of it, closed her mouth and returned to staring at her feet, arms folded.

"Melody, we don't force anyone to share," said the heavy-set, blonde lady. "When Julia feels like sharing, she will."

"That ain't even her real name!" Melody continued. "I called her name three times last meeting; she didn't even bat an eyelid."

"She can use any name she wishes," the heavy-set blonde lady offered.

"Well, I don't think it's right! Here we all are, spilling our guts, and she just sits there." Melody's head was starting to bob as she talked. "She needs to say how she feels."

"You want to know how I feel?" Margo asked.

"Yes, I do," Melody replied, head bobbing.

"You really want to know?" Margo reiterated.

"Yes, I do," Melody repeated.

"Okay, I'll tell you." Margo stood up. She pointed in Doug's direction. "I feel like taking a baseball bat and beating the bastard who raped his seventy-three-year-old mother to death. I feel like locking the piece of shit who murdered her daughter and raped her granddaughter in a room with a pack of starving pit bulls, with two pounds of liver wrapped round his neck, and watching through the window." she said, nodding in Georgia's direction. She gestured toward the young Hispanic man. "I feel like chaining the assholes that gang-banged Raul's sister to the back of my truck and driving thirty miles an hour through the desert, because forty–five would be too fast, and they'd die too fucking quickly!" Her breath was coming in short pants, her face reddening. "I want to get the guy who killed her husband," she said pointing to the Hispanic lady, "and blow his fucking brains out! I want to find the piece of crap that broke into your house in the middle of the night and stabbed your husband to death, and do the same to him. I want to get the guy who shot your son!" she said, pointing at an older couple, and then began going around the circle in order. "The animal who stole your little girl out of her bed in the middle of the night; the gang member who shot your kid on his way home from school; the piece of filth who took your eight-year-old son off a swing set in broad daylight," she paused and took a deep breath. "I want to kill the bastard who killed my daughter, only they don't know who did it! I don't know if they'll ever know! They won't even tell me how she died, because it's an 'ongoing investigation," she said making quotation signs in the air. "I want to make someone pay for the agony I go through every day of my life! I don't want to share, I don't want to heal, and I will never, ever, fucking forgive! *That's* how I feel!"

Margo stood in the center of the circle of chairs. She was visibly shaking as she looked around at the astonished faces. The room was silent, apart from the sound of Margo's rapid breathing. All eyes were on her, every mouth open in total and complete shock.

"Well. Hmm. Okay. I think that's enough for tonight everyone. I'll see you all on Friday." The heavy-set blonde lady looked very uncomfortable.

Chapter Eleven

Margo poured herself a third cup of coffee from the large urn in the corner of the room. These meetings lasted only two hours, and yet she drank more coffee at one than she did all day at home. She added the powdered creamer and sugar as quietly as she could and tossed the stirrer into the trash can, already filled to the brim with empty polystyrene cups. Apparently the people in the earlier meetings drank just as much coffee as her group. Carefully, she tiptoed back to her seat, trying hard not to disturb the present speaker.

Melody dabbed the tissue to her eye and sniffed. "You know, I've been a 9-1-1 dispatcher for eight years. I've had to go through therapy four times for various reasons related to my job. I've had people die while they were talking to me. I've had people who killed other people while they were talking to me. I had to stay calm, keep them calm. I had to stay in control of the situation. I knew it was a stressful job going in. I just never thought that I would ever hear someone calling for help from my own home. I wasn't prepared for that. When my next door neighbor called to say there had been some kind of altercation next door and her neighbor had been stabbed, I prayed it was on the other side. When she gave the apartment number I actually started to scream. With all my experience and training, I couldn't hold it together. Another dispatcher had to take over. To this day, I hate myself for not being able to help my husband."

"Do you think you could have saved him?" the heavy-set, blonde lady asked.

"No. He had been stabbed thirty-six times; twenty-seven times in the chest alone. Both lungs were collapsed, and his heart had been pierced five times. The dispatcher was trying to talk my neighbor through CPR, but there was too much blood in his airway and lungs. He was pronounced dead at the scene."

"So why do you hate yourself? What could you have done?" Georgia asked.

"Nothing. I think that's it. I was of no use at all." Melody rubbed her enlarged abdomen. "I just don't know what I'm going to tell this little one."

"Tell him the truth. Some sick, drug-crazed maniac broke in and killed his dad while he slept. What else does he need to know? He still has you." Margo didn't mean to sound so matter-of-fact.

"Yes, he does," Melody beamed. "After he's born, I think I'll be ready to go back to work. My mother's going to help me out. I'm going to work the day shift. That will be better for me. Not as much crime through the day. Mostly heart attacks and car crashes. You know, cheerful shit." Everyone in the room smiled.

"Okay, everyone. I think this session is over," the heavy-set blonde said. "I will see you all Tuesday evening. Have a safe and enjoyable weekend."

Have a safe and enjoyable weekend. Margo repeated the words in her head. She looked around the room. They had all lost someone special to violent crimes. Could any of them ever really feel safe again? It was hard to even think of enjoying herself anymore. There was not much left in Margo's life that she considered enjoyable. The shrink had ordered her to attend this class for six months. She had unwillingly obliged, and had completed four of the six already. It wasn't so bad. The meetings were held every Tuesday and Friday evening at seven p.m. like clockwork. It was funny; she felt a lot better after her maniacal rant a few weeks ago. At least she could talk about it a little now. Here anyway. At home she preferred to steer clear of the subject of Cassidy's murder. In fact, she barely spoke at all at home. *Poor Carla,* thought Margo, she had suppressed her grief to be there for Margo, a fact Margo was very much aware of. And yet, Margo wasn't there for Carla; she couldn't be. She found it hard to be there for anyone. Jim called her daily, much to the chagrin of Brigitte. He appeared to be genuinely concerned about her. He ought to be, they had been together for twenty-three years. She wondered if he would stay with Brigitte that long. Nah! Brigitte would dump him for someone younger way before then.

Margo exited the building and perused the parking lot in search of her black BMW. It was still light out, a pleasant, but breezy, evening. She shivered a little as she pulled her pale blue cardigan around her shoulders. It was cool out for June. Summer would be late this year, she thought.

"Excuse me; Julia?" The Hispanic lady seemed a little timid around Margo. "A few of us are going for coffee; would you like to join us?"

"Thank you, but no," Margo replied. "I need something a little stronger than coffee." Margo began rummaging around in her purse for car keys.

Pietra Alvera nodded, smiled, and turned to leave. She turned back to Margo suddenly. "You know," she said, "I haven't had a drink since Chico died. Would you like to go with me for a glass of wine or two?"

"Okay," said Margo, "but I have to drive. I am a lousy passenger."

The two drove in Margo's car to a small Italian restaurant a few blocks from the counseling center. There were still quite a few people waiting for tables, even though it was well after nine p.m. They ordered appetizers and red wine at the bar.

"I came here once or twice with Chico," Pietra said.

"Oh, I'm sorry. Would you rather go somewhere else?" Margo was genuinely apologetic for her choice of venue.

"Oh no! Please! We always ate out. We ran a Latin dance school not too far from here. We didn't close the school until ten at night, so we would eat at whichever place was open. I think we ate in every restaurant in L.A." Pietra looked around, apparently savoring the memory. Margo noticed for the first time how attractive she was. Her hair was pulled back in a tight bun, which aged her a little, but Margo could see now that she was no older than early forties. Her face was free of wrinkles, and if it were not for the dark circles under her eyes she could easily pass for mid-thirties.

"Oh, my God! Chico Alvera!" Margo suddenly realized that she knew Pietra's murdered husband. "I took salsa lessons with him."

"Yes, Margo, I remember." Pietra squeezed her hand.

"You've known who I am all along?" Margo said surprised.

"Not all along. I recognized you when you went crazy that night." Pietra started laughing. "I know it's harder on you, because everybody knows your business. I didn't want to add to it. So I'll call you Julia in front of the others. The horned-rimmed glasses are a great touch, though. They make you look like a school teacher."

"Yes, they do make me look smart, don't they?" Margo laughed, removing the glasses and placing them on the table before her. "They're just plain glass, for appearances only. I'm really quite dim."

"I don't believe that. Chico said you were a very savvy lady. He was so impressed with you." Pietra raised her glass in salute.

"Pietra, I'm so sorry. Chico was a wonderful man." Margo felt guilty somehow for not recognizing her earlier.

"Please, my friends call me Peta." She had a wonderful smile, Margo thought. It was a shame that she didn't smile much anymore. "Yes, he was wonderful. You should have seen him twenty-four years ago when we came from Brazil. Chico had won his green card in a raffle and had to be in the states by July seventeenth. My twenty-first birthday was on the fourteenth, so we got a permit on my birthday, and got married in Rio de Janiero the same day. We spent the next day at the American embassy to get my visa, and flew to the states two days later."

"That was a little traumatic."

"Oh, you don't know. My father hated Chico, who was a dancer in one of the shows in Rio. In my father's eyes he was a gigolo. He forbade me to see him. He told me he would kill him if he found out I was still seeing him," Peta laughed. "Luckily, he won the immigration lottery, and we had a way out! So we eloped to America."

"That is so romantic!" Margo squealed.

"I don't know about romantic!" Peta smiled. "We worked every minute we could. Chico worked construction through the day while I worked at a shoe factory. We gave dance lessons in the early evenings at a local dance school, and danced three nights a week at one of the Latin nightclubs in town. At one point I weighed ninety-seven pounds. I think I forgot to eat, or maybe I just didn't have time. Anyway, after two years, we finally had enough money to open our own school. We both quit our day jobs and the other dance school. We kept dancing at the nightclub, though. It was good advertising. It paid off. So how did you get your big break?"

Margo raised her eyebrows and shrugged. "I slept with the director." Both women burst out laughing.

"Excuse me. Miss Priestley?" A meek-looking, skinny woman with wrinkled clothing stood beside Margo. "Do you think I could get a picture with you, please?"

"Certainly!" Margo answered with a genuine smile. She gently placed her arm around the woman's shoulders and smiled brightly at the instant camera held by the woman's equally skinny and wrinkled-looking husband.

"Thank you so much! I wasn't sure it was you until you took your glasses off!" The woman beamed and walked away quickly. "I told you it was her!" she admonished her husband.

"That doesn't bother you?" Peta asked.

"Used to it," Margo replied, shrugging. "Hats and sun glasses are normally enough to let me run around town unnoticed. That, and an unlimited array of wigs."

"I don't think I would like that," Peta said truthfully.

"Oh, it has its perks," Margo said, smiling at the bartender, who had written the word 'complimentary' on the top of the check.

It was raining lightly when they left the restaurant. Both women ran laughing to the car. Peta was good company. Margo had enjoyed their time together immensely. They drove back to the counseling center in good spirits. The restaurant had proven to be way more therapeutic than the support group.

The center was not in the nicest part of town. 'Ladies of the night' adorned many of the corners, while young men with various 'items for sale' meandered in and out of the shadows. The two women commented light-heartedly on the various outfits being paraded before them. They oohed and aahed in disbelief at the total lack of modesty of most of the women. A young boy approached the car with a spray bottle and a fistful of crumpled newspaper when they stopped at a light. Margo shook her head and waved him away. There was no way she was going to roll down her window to give him a couple of dollars in this neighborhood.

"Oh, my God!" Peta exclaimed. She was staring down a narrow street to their right. A couple was having intercourse in the shadows. The woman was up against the wall, the man pushed up against her, his left arm across her neck. "These people are animals!" she spat. "Why can't they go somewhere private to do that?"

Margo was relieved when the light changed to green. "Some people just don't have any morals," she said as the car pulled away. The vision of the man's arm across the woman's throat popped back into her head. Instantaneously, the two women looked at each other with the same expression of realization. "He's raping her!" Margo gasped. She quickly checked her rear-view and turned the wheel to the left as fast as she could.

"Margo, what are you doing?" Peta shouted. "Let's just call the police."

"What if he kills her?" Margo shouted back, completing the U-turn. "There's no time!" She pushed her foot hard onto the accelerator. She quickly made the turn into the narrow street and screeched to a halt. In the headlights stood a Hispanic man with a young black girl, no more than twenty. The look of horror on the girl's face confirmed their suspicions. Something glinted in his right hand — a knife. The man turned suddenly, pushing the young woman to the ground. He stood in front of the car. Surprisingly, he didn't run off. He stood there staring at the two women. A hand went down to his groin. He grabbed hold of his appendage proudly, while wielding the knife with his other hand.

"You want some of this, bitch?" he shouted to Margo. "Get out the car, bitch!"

Margo looked at the young black girl on the floor. She was inching her way backward, putting space between herself and her assailant. The man's eyes followed Margo's. He screamed at the girl.

"Who told you to move? You fucking stay there!" He turned his attention back to the car. "You better get the fuck outa here!" he yelled.

Margo looked at Peta. She knew as soon as they left he would go after the girl again. What the hell were they supposed to do?

"You hear me, bitch?" he screamed at Margo. "I'm tellin' you, bitch, I'll fuck you up!"

"What do we do?" Margo shrieked.

"Hit him!" Peta answered through clenched teeth.

The two women exchanged glances. Margo nodded. She stamped her foot hard onto the gas. The car lurched forward, coming to an abrupt stop at the wall, pinning the man. Margo swore she felt the crushing of bone through the metal. The attacker fell forward. He slumped over the hood of the car as the two women stared in disbelief. His eyes were open, staring. Blood trickled from his nostrils and open mouth. One of his hands trembled violently against the hood of the car, and his eyes suddenly rolled back in his head. Then his torso relaxed totally as the last breath of life escaped from his gaping mouth. To the right of the car the young girl rose quickly, turned, and ran up the narrow street, vanishing into the shadows. Margo was frozen, her fingers wrapped tightly around the mahogany steering wheel.

"We have to get out of here, Margo," Peta said. "Now!"

Margo stared at the scene before her. What the hell had just happened? The blood from the man's nose looked black under the street light. In fact the whole picture appeared to be in black and white, like she was watching it on TV, instead of through her windshield.

"Margo!" Peta shouted. "We have to get out of here!"

Silently, Margo put the car into reverse and slowly drew back. The man's lifeless body fell to the ground. Without turning around, Margo backed the battered nose of the car toward the main road. There was no one on the street. Quickly she made the turn and accelerated into the darkness.

Chapter Twelve

Peta blinked at the sunlight streaking through the patio windows. She sat up slowly, taking in the unfamiliar surroundings. This was a beautiful room. If this were a hotel, this room would cost a fortune, she thought. She ran her hand over the beige satin pillowcase. The color palette was a little too neutral for her Latin taste, but she could definitely get used to the luxury. The memory of the night before came rushing back.

"Oh, my God!" she sighed.

She rose from the bed and picked up a folded robe from a nearby chair. She shook it open and pulled it on over the bra and panties she had slept in, while slipping her feet into plush terry slippers. Hesitantly, she headed through the door into the hallway. The smell of coffee was coming from somewhere in the house. She walked silently toward a staircase at the end of the hallway. Someone was softly singing down there. Margo? It sounded cheerful. She doubted it was Margo.

She navigated the stairs without a sound, thanks to the plush carpeting. From the bottom step she could see an archway that led into the kitchen. She headed in that direction.

"Good morning!" said a freckle-faced woman with short curly brown hair. "I'm Carla. Margo said you'd be up soon. Can I fix you some breakfast? The coffee's already made, or would you prefer tea?" She smiled warmly.

"No breakfast for me, but black coffee would be perfect. Thank you." She returned Carla's smile. "Is Margo around?"

"She took her coffee down to the beach." Carla held out a mug of steaming coffee, nodding toward a half-open barn door. "Be careful on the stairs. They're cut out of the cliff so they're not perfectly even."

Peta accepted her coffee and graciously excused herself. She paused on the patio just outside the back door. She stared in disbelief at Margo's backyard, the Pacific Ocean. To her left the patio curved around to the main patio and swimming pool. She knew that because her room overlooked it. Below the pool area was a private cove probably accessible only by boat or the stairway that led from the house. Across the sandy cove stretched a volleyball net. Peta couldn't imagine Margo playing volleyball. She assumed that Cassidy and her friends had probably hung out there when she was home. She imagined how painful memories of that might be to Margo. To her right was the staircase carved out of the rock, which led down to a second beach area. She took hold of the wrought iron rail and slowly started her descent. Halfway down the stairs was a level area with a bench and a standpipe for rinsing off your feet on the way up, Peta assumed. She removed her clean, terry slippers and placed them on the bench. She wasn't going to be remembered as "the woman who walked sand into the plush white rugs." She resumed her descent to the sandy cove below her.

Margo was nowhere to be seen. The sand was fine, and Peta sank into it, feeling a little unsteady on her feet. She was in a small cove with little view of the beach. It was almost like a huge cave with no ceiling. Looking around she saw small speakers concealed within the rocky walls. She envisioned a huge bonfire burning in the center with loud music. This would be an awesome place for a beach barbecue. Looking up she could see blue sky. The daylight illuminated the cove, but no sunlight entered. Peta shivered. It was extremely cool in here; she headed toward the beach.

Exiting the cove, Margo came into full view. She was standing in the surf. She wore a pale blue, sheer negligee set, which moved lightly around her in the breeze, emphasizing her slender yet shapely physique. Her thick red hair was loose and wavy. No wonder she was a movie star, Peta thought. She really was quite beautiful. Margo nursed a coffee mug in her hands, apparently deep in thought. She raised it to take a sip.

"Margo?" Peta was careful not to surprise her.

"Hey there!" She smiled warmly at Peta, walking slowly toward her. "How did you sleep?" Margo shook her head softly and sighed. "I'm sorry, stupid question. I guess I'm stuck in small-talk mode. I had to act as though everything was fine for Carla."

"What did you tell her?" Peta was intrigued.

"Oh, my God! Absolutely nothing!" Margo stared out at the ocean. She sighed again. "Peta?"

"Yes?"

"I have a really great lawyer. He'll do anything for me. If anyone can get me out of this, he can." She smiled gently and looked down at the sand. "I'm going to tell him I was alone last night."

"What? Why? Are you crazy?" Peta's accent was more pronounced when she became agitated. "You're turning yourself in?"

"I have to," Margo replied adamantly. "My car is an absolute mess. It's totalled, and there's blood all over it. I'm sure the police have been pulling paint chips galore out of the guy I crushed last night. I don't really know what the hell else to do."

"I'm going with you then!" Peta folded her arms defiantly. "I will be able to back up your story."

"Peta! We left the scene of an accident!" Margo stated earnestly. "We should have reported it last night!"

"Margo!" Peta said mockingly. "You aimed your car at the guy! It wasn't an accident!"

"We saved that girl's life!" Margo wailed defensively.

"What girl, Margo? Where is she?" Peta held her hands up in despair. "We can't prove there was anyone else there!"

"There's forensics!" Margo snapped back. "They can find evidence on his … his ... penis!"

"What penis?" Peta fired back. "You crushed it!"

Both women collapsed into uncontrollable fits of laughter at this point. Tears ran down Margo's face, and she clutched her sides as she bent over seemingly in pain.

"Stop it!" Peta shrieked, trying to regain her composure. "It's not funny!" She was laughing silently now. The kind of laugh that won't quit until it's run its course; the kind of laugh that hurts.

The two women stood there for what seemed an eternity laughing. As one stopped, the other started, which in turn would start the other off again. Finally they regained control of themselves and sat down on the sand.

"We have to fix the car," Peta said finally.

"I can't take that into a shop!" Margo whined.

"I don't mean fix it; I mean *fix it*," Peta said matter-of-factly. "I think I know someone who can help us."

"Who?" Margo demanded.

"I've been going for coffee with Doug after the meetings," Peta said shyly.

"Doug?" Margo queried. "The fire-fighter guy?"

"He's a fire marshal," Peta said defensively. "He might be able to help us." She stared intently at Margo. "Do you think you can get rid of Marla for a couple of hours?"

"Her name's Carla, and actually, she's leaving this afternoon to visit her daughter for a week."

"Perfect," said Peta. She rose and turned toward the stairs leading to the house. "I'll be back."

"You're going to call him now?" Margo looked at her watch. It was only seven-fifteen.

"No," Peta said. "I'm going to get my coffee. I left it on the bench."

Chapter Thirteen

Doug whistled loudly. He crouched down to get a better look at the damage. "Wow!" He inspected the grill, or what was left of it. "Whoa!" he said, shaking his head.

"Oh, for God's sake, Doug, would you say something intelligible?" Margo was pacing around the garage frantically.

"You must have creamed this guy!" he stated unnecessarily. His eyes perused the heavy bloodstains.

"Thank you for stating the obvious," Margo snapped impatiently.

"I just can't believe you did this!" he said standing. "Well, Margo maybe, but you, Peta? I'm in shock." Margo rolled her eyes.

"It was necessary," Peta said softly.

"Oh, I'm not judging you!" Doug smiled. "I'm sure the bastard deserved it. I'm just surprised, that's all."

"So, what now?" Margo sighed. "God, this is such a mess. We shouldn't have involved you, Doug. I'm so sorry."

"Hey, it's not over till the fat fireman sings," Doug joked. "I need to call in a few favors." He pulled his cell phone out of his pants pocket. "We have to get rid of this car," he said, looking over at his large truck. "I have chains with me, so I can take it now, but I need to hose this thing down. I don't want to tow it across town covered in blood. It's better if you two stay here. I'd rather you didn't hear or see who I have to deal with, and I really don't want them to see Margo. She's a little too famous, and they don't need to know any names."

"Money's no object." She pulled a wad of hundred-dollar bills from her pocket. "This is all I have on me, but I can get a lot more if you need it." She held the money out toward Doug, who accepted it readily.

"This will definitely help," he said flicking through the bills. "Wow, this is more than enough."

"We'll be in the house if you need us; you have the number," Margo muttered, pulling Peta along behind her.

~

Margo and Peta sprang to their feet when they heard the front door softly click closed. Doug walked into the kitchen. He nodded toward the coffee pot.

"Any left in there?"

"I'm making a fresh pot," Margo said.

"No. No. I'll make it!" Peta gently pushed Margo out of the way. "I'm sorry, Margo, but now I know why you have a housekeeper." Margo frowned.

"Thanks, Peta." Doug smiled warmly at her. He perched on one of the tall stools at the granite island. "Well, it's gone," he declared. "If anyone should ask about your car, it was destroyed in a garage fire about three months ago. I'll be able to give you an exact date when I check my calendar at the office. I was the fire marshal who inspected the damage, so I just have to add it in wherever it will fit. I think it was faulty wiring, or maybe a small rodent chewed through a wire. I haven't decided yet, I'll let you know. Funny coincidence how we met later at the support group, huh?" He shrugged his big shoulders. "You never called the fire department because you managed to put the fire out with extinguishers. Stupid, but very brave on your part. So there won't be any collaborating 9-1-1 tapes. There was minimal damage to the garage, but the car was a write-off. I have a friend in the insurance company. You should be receiving your check in the mail sometime next week. Your claim will be dated the day after my visit."

"But what about my insurance company?" Margo interrupted.

"Relax," Doug replied. "You're in good hands," he said with a wink. "This is the company that did the repairs to the garage." He pulled the pink copy of a work inventory from his back pocket. Sadly, this company went out of business two months ago, so they won't be able to verify that they did the work. That's a shame. After the insurance company wrote your car off, it was taken to a dump just outside town where it was immediately stripped of any useable parts and crushed shortly thereafter, but you wouldn't even know or care about that. Is that coffee ready yet?"

Peta emerged from behind the counter, holding a mug toward Doug. He accepted it gratefully and took a sip. "Did I forget anything, Margo?" he asked.

Margo blinked. "I ... Er ... What? ... How? ... " she mumbled.

"Oh, for God's sake, Margo!" Peta said, handing her a mug. "Would you say something intelligible?"

Chapter Fourteen

Georgia Franklin was angry. Her lips were drawn together in a straight line, and her arms were folded tightly across her chest. Margo could see more than that in her eyes though. There was definitely sorrow there, and fear. She had sat silent for most of the meeting.

"Georgia, is there something you would like to get off your chest?' The heavy-set blonde lady asked. Her look was one of genuine concern.

"No, Audrey," she replied calmly. "I don't think there's much point, but thank you for your concern." She went back to her tight-lipped stance.

"Is that asshole out of prison yet?" Margo asked coolly. Peta shot her a look with wide eyes and raised eyebrows. "What?" Margo asked defensively. "I only asked."

"Friday," Georgia answered meekly.

"So what are you going to do?" Margo continued. "You can't just let him take her."

"I don't know. I only have twelve thousand. That's with the six-hundred and fifty-three dollars the neighbors collected, too. It's not even half. It doesn't matter now anyway." She sighed heavily.

"There's no way you can get out of there?" Melody asked.

"There's a car parked at the front, and one at the side of the building, to make sure I don't go down the fire escape." She wrung her hands nervously. "They follow us to the school every morning, and home every afternoon; when I go to the grocery store, to the park, even to church. Can you believe it? They even come into the church to make sure I don't hand her off to someone!"

"I'll give you the money," Margo said. "I can write you a check right now." She looked around the room. "I … er … came into a little money."

"Uh huh?" Melody teased. "Would that be for endangered species?" She said turning to Doug on her left. "I prefer the one about the brothel madam, though. I saw that one twice." She smiled smugly.

Margo stared hard at Peta. "Hey!" Peta cried. "I didn't tell them. They knew all the time. You think I'm the only one who goes to the movies!"

Margo shrugged. "So do you want the money?" she asked.

"Thank you, Ju … I mean Margo," she said politely. "That won't be necessary.'

"Why not? You don't have to pay it back," Margo persisted.

"He doesn't want the money anymore," Georgia answered. "I got a visit from his henchmen this morning. They said Mr. Moon no longer wants to sell his property. He'll be by Friday afternoon to pick up his belongings." She looked resolved to accept her hopeless situation.

"You can't just let him take her!" Margo shrieked. "That's insane!"

"What choice do I have? He'll kill us both." She raised her index finger as if she had had some kind of revelation. "I will borrow that money from you. Maybe if he sees the cash, he'll change his mind."

"No," said Melody. "He won't. This guy is a pedophile and a murderer. He raises dogs to fight to the death. He sells drugs to kids. This guy enjoys seeing pain. He doesn't need your money. He doesn't want your money. He wants your granddaughter."

"Can't you hide her somewhere in the building?" Margo was determined to find a solution.

"My building is being bought by a supermarket chain," Georgia answered. "As the apartments become vacant, they're boarded up. At the moment I don't think we have a third of the apartments occupied. My neighbors on the left of me moved out the day before yesterday. They'll be by the first of next month to board it up, along with the other two in the building that became empty this month. They don't want homeless people moving in. The people who are left in the building don't want anything to do with Mr. Moon. Do you know what he would do to them if he caught them hiding Monique? It's hopeless."

"We can't let this happen. We have to do something!" Margo's eyes looked beseechingly around the room. She stared directly at Doug.

"Why are you looking at me?" Doug looked very uncomfortable.

"We have to do something," Margo looked from face to face. "How long are we going to be victims? How long are we going to take this shit? We have to do something."

"Er ... Margo?" Audrey interrupted. "I think this is a matter for the police; don't you?" This was the most nervous Margo had ever seen her.

"Don't worry, Audrey," Margo cooed. "We're not going to do anything illegal."

Chapter Fifteen

"Hi, my name's Maggie. Can I get your drink order?" The waitress was a very well-endowed, pretty blonde. Yet another Hollywood hopeful, Margo speculated.

"I'll have a regular coffee with cream," said Doug.

"Make that two, please," Peta added.

"Oh, I can't drink regular coffee at this time. I'll be up all night," Georgia said, looking at her watch. "Can I get a decaf, please?"

"I'll just take a water; thanks," Melody smiled.

"I'd like a Jack and ginger." Margo noticed the others were staring at her. "Hey!" she said; "I need one!"

"You know what?" Doug held up his hand. "I'll take one of those also."

"Me, too," Peta chimed.

"Oh, I can't drink that stuff." Georgia wrinkled her nose. "I'll have a Vodka martini."

"I'm fine with the water," Melody reiterated, patting her swollen abdomen.

They sat there silently, waiting for the waitress to bring their order. Nobody wanted to be the first to speak. The atmosphere was strained, awkward. The dim lighting helped to shield the mixture of anxiety, embarrassment, and shame evident on each of the faces around the table. They were there for a reason, a horrible reason. They were planning a murder. Not a bad murder though; a justifiable murder. A necessary murder.

Maggie returned with the drinks. Margo held out her credit card to the waitress. "Can we start a tab, please?"

"I've got this." Doug pushed Margo's hand back and placed his own card on the tray.

"Would you like to look at the menu? The kitchen's still open," Maggie said cheerfully.

"No, drinks are sufficient." Doug was anxious to have her leave.

"Do you have chicken wings?" Georgia asked.

Margo gave her the big-eyed, high eye-browed, shut-up look. Her palms held up. What kind of murder squad was this?

"Oh, okay. Never mind." She flapped to the waitress. Maggie finally left the table and headed toward the bar.

Margo waited for the waitress to get out of earshot. "So Georgia, you're absolutely certain the apartment next to you is empty."

"I'm positive." Georgia leaned in to the table. "I don't know how we're going to get in, though. We're going to need a key."

"Don't worry about that," Doug said. "I can open it." Margo shot him a look that said she wondered how he knew how to open locks. "I'm a fireman, Margo. We have tools to get into anything." Margo looked somewhat relieved.

"How many times have Moon's thugs been to your apartment?" Margo sipped her drink.

"Just the two times. This morning, and the one time a few months ago." Georgia nodded her head in assurance.

"That might pose a problem." Doug rubbed his chin. "How many apartments in the hallway?"

"There are four doors on either side. I'm the second one down on the right."

"They would remember that," Doug said shaking his head. "They're going to realize it's the wrong apartment."

"Oh, no. They won't come up," Georgia said with conviction.

"What do you mean? How do you know that?" Peta asked.

"Well, for a start, he's not going to call off the watchdogs, in case I slip out. Then there's this little show he likes to put on," Georgia rolled her eyes.

"What show?" Melody suddenly showed interest.

"He has this real fancy walking cane. It has a real big moonstone in the handle and brass on the tip." Georgia rolled her eyes again and tutted. "His big thing is intimidation. So when he comes to pay a visit he taps the end of his cane on the sidewalk as he walks. That way you know he's coming so you can get good and scared before he gets there. And he always has that ugly damn dog with him. You know you're either going to get shot, beat with the stick, or ripped to shreds by that ugly damn dog."

"Does he still have the dog?" Margo asked. "I mean, he's still in prison. Where's the dog now?"

"My neighbor told me his sister has all of them at her place in Venice Beach. He said she keeps the white one in the house with her, and she has the other two in kennels in the back yard. She can't keep them all together because they get too mean and pack up. They nearly ripped her to pieces once. Apparently she lost some fingers and her face got messed up."

"And she didn't get rid of them after that?" Melody was in shock.

"She might be his sister, but he'd beat her to death before he'd let those dogs go. They're worth a fortune as fighters; they just can't be together. The white one's the worst. That dog won't quit once it gets a hold of you, and it would love to get a hold of Moon. He beat the hell out of it every day, just to make it mean; had to keep a muzzle on it all the time. He only took the muzzle of when it was eating, fighting, or attacking."

"Wow!" Said Peta. "Not even his own dog likes him."

"None of them do," Georgia continued. "I think they'd tear him to pieces if they could."

"See, everyone wants to kill this guy," Doug added.

"But that would be illegal, wouldn't it?" said a deep voice from the next table.

Moses Jackson sat a few feet from them. He took a swig from his open Corona. He was an extremely quiet member of the group. In fact, Margo didn't realize he was there most of the time until the end of the session when he would always volunteer to escort the ladies to their cars. He was a retired L.A.P.D officer. His career had been cut short by a .35 caliber bullet that had shattered his left kneecap, leaving him with a distinct limp and a fat disability pension. Margo wasn't really sure why he was in the group. He had been attending for a long time and tended to listen more than share. He was often looked to for legal advice by the others. He'd been missing the last couple of weeks, but now he was back and apparently listening more than ever.

"Moses," Doug acknowledged.

"Doug; ladies," Moses raised his bottle. The women smiled their hellos.

"Been there long?" Doug asked.

"Long enough."

"We haven't said anything incriminating," Margo said sipping her Jack and ginger.

"Who said you did? I'm just sitting here minding my own business, waiting for my wife to pick me up. She finishes her shift at ten. My car's broke." He took a sip from his bottle. "Yep. She works the late shift." He raised one eyebrow. "Los Angeles County Animal Control."

Margo turned to Doug just in time to see a huge smile spread across his face.

Chapter Sixteen

"I told you I don't know!" Delia Haines wiped the blood from her lip with the back of her hand.

"You're telling me you didn't hear nuthin? You didn't hear those goddamn dogs barkin'." He punched her again hard in the face.

"They didn't bark!' she protested. "Whoever took them must have drugged them or something!" She folded her arms over her head for protection. Her knees were pulled up tight over her abdomen. The fetal position didn't save her, however. He kicked her as hard as he could in the back.

The pit bull in the corner was going crazy, straining at the leash AJ Lewis held. He was not happy about the way his former master was beating his present mistress mercilessly. This was one strong damn dog. AJ weighed in at two-hundred and thirty pounds and stood six-feet-four inches tall, yet controlling this dog was an effort. He suffered in silence. He was not about to say anything to enrage Moon more, if that was possible.

"I told you to watch my fuckin' dogs!" he yelled, kicking her again. "What were you doing? Smokin' shit?"

"I was sleeping! They came in the night!" She was sobbing now.

"Who bought you this goddamn house?" he yelled.

"You did, Delroy."

"Who paid for you to put your punk ass kids in that fancy private school?"

"You did, Delroy."

"Who got rid of that piece of shit man of yours when he didn't do right by you?"

"You did, Delroy."

"And this ... is how ... you repay me?" he said, kicking her again and again in synchronization with his words. "When I come back, I'm throwing your ass out on the street if you're still here!" He spat. He spun around. "Where's my goddamn stick?" He strode over to the corner where his moonstone-topped walking cane was leaned against the wall. He pointed the tip of it at the dog's face. Its lips curled back exposing large white teeth. "Get a muzzle on that thing and get in the car!" He turned to his sister. "I'll be back in two hours. Make sure you're out of here."

Delia Haines rose and staggered to the window in time to see AJ climb into the back of the car with the dog and Moon take his place behind the wheel. She tasted the blood running from her nose to the corner of her mouth, and once again wiped it with the back of her hand. She sobbed loudly. She looked down at the mutilated remains of her left hand. Her other hand went up to gently caress the disfiguring scars that ran the length of the right side of her face. His fault, all of it. He had taken her life and controlled her like a puppet. He had told their mama before she died that he would take care of her, but he had lied. He had beaten her, abused her both mentally and sexually, whored her out to numerous men, killed the man she loved, and now he was throwing her into the streets, scarred, torn, and twisted.

"I hope you die, you piece of shit," she whispered as the car pulled away.

Chapter Seventeen

"Hurry up! He's on his way!" Margo snapped the phone shut. "He'll be here in ten minutes."

Doug gave the screwdriver another quick turn. He wiped the brass numbers on the door with a handkerchief, which he then placed in his pocket. "Okay, all done here!"

"Georgia? Are you ready?" she called across the room.

"Oh, my God! Was that Melody on the phone already?" Georgia looked nervous.

"Don't panic! We'll be right next door. Remember, when you're ready, thump on the wall. Then get the hell out!" Margo looked deeply into Georgia's eyes. "We'll be right next door." She hugged Georgia tightly, and hurried through the open door. Georgia closed it behind her.

Georgia walked to the window. Sure enough, there was the Hummer that had sat there for the last five weeks. She knew the black '85 Cadillac Seville was in place at the side of the building, guarding the fire escape. She had checked on it a dozen times already. She exhaled loudly. No turning back now. She took a seat in the armchair and ran her finger along the design in the fabric. This was a good choice, she thought. This was definitely the kind of furniture she would have picked. It was a little pricier than she would have chosen, especially seeing as nobody was ever going to use it again. The chink of metal on tile broke her concentration. She looked up. There it was again — and again. *Tap, tap, tap.*

"He's here," She said in a whisper. She felt the air leave her lungs. They were right. The noise of the cane on the ground did instill fear. Her heart began to race. "Stay calm," she told herself.

Tap, tap, tap. It was louder now, closer. *Tap, tap.* It stopped. Georgia rose from the chair. She stared at the front door, waiting. Although fully prepared, when Moon thumped loudly on the door, Georgia jumped. She gasped for air, and then exhaled slowly as she regained control of her emotions. Slowly she approached the front door.

"Hello?" she called out, trying to sound as normal as possible. She didn't know why. Who the hell could sound normal while giving up their eleven-year-old granddaughter to a murderous pedophile?

"Open up, old lady," Moon ordered.

"Disrespectful little punk!" Georgia thought. She was only fifty-two. Who the hell was he calling old lady? She opened the door slowly. "Come in, Mr. Moon."

Moon stepped through the door, the white pit beside him. The dog growled through the muzzle. Moon gave him a sharp rap with the stick. "Shut up!" he snarled. He eyed her rubber cleaning gloves with distaste.

"Oh, excuse me," Georgia offered, "the toilet was blocked."

"Where's the girl?" Moon looked angry. "I don't have all day."

"She was a little upset. I made her lay down." Georgia nodded toward a door at the end of a short, narrow hallway. "I'll fetch her," she said solemnly, walking toward the room. Moon took a step after her. "Please, Mr. Moon," she pleaded, "she's upset enough as it is. Please. Let me wake her." He nodded his assent.

Georgia slowly walked up the hallway. She tapped softly on the door. "Monique, honey," she said, opening the door slowly; "it's time." She vanished behind the bedroom door. Once inside the room she exhaled heavily. She had been careful not to open the door too widely, exposing the empty room inside, devoid of furniture, soft furnishings, and eleven-year-old girls. She walked quickly over to the window and slid it open, before rapping sharply on the wall.

Byron Lewis leaned forward to stare out the windshield of the black Cadillac Seville. "What the hell is that?" he said excitedly. "The old lady's climbing out the fuckin' window, man!"

"No, man. That's not her window!" Lamont Washington counted windows in from the right side of the building. He'd sat behind the wheel in this car watching her apartment long enough to know which one was hers. "That's not her window! Something's going on!" He frantically pulled his cell phone from his pocket and flipped it open.

Suddenly the rear passenger side door opened and Byron felt something cold and hard press into the base of his skull.

"Tell your friend to close his phone. Tell him now."

Byron assessed the situation as well as he was able. He was probably going to die anyway, either at the hands of this motherfucker in the back seat, or the motherfucker in the building. The one in the building would make it slow, real slow.

"Dial the fucking number!" The windshield suddenly dripped crimson. The smell of sulphur filled the car. Lamont Washington froze.

"Close the phone and pass it to me." Moses was calm and collected. He didn't need to waste words. His actions spoke volumes. "Pass me the goddamn phone, now," he said sternly. He held out a hand, his other one holding the gun pointed in Lamont's direction.

Lamont's hand shook as he closed the flip phone. "Take it easy, man. I'll give you the fucking phone. Just take it easy." Shaking, he placed the phone into Moses' outstretched fingers. "We cool, we …" He fell silent. The small red hole in the front of his head did not reflect the damage the bullet caused exiting the back.

"Next time choose your fucking friends better," Moses said, sliding toward the driver's side rear door. Ensuring that he was not visible from the front parking lot, he slowly got out of the car and walked to the back of the building.

~

Angel Griffin cranked up the volume when his favorite track came on. If you were going to play rap you had to play it loud. The bass had to shake the glass in the doors. You had to feel it through the seat. It was the law. The Hummer was the ideal vehicle for rap. It literally bounced to the beat.

"Turn the motherfucking music down!" Jerome Jackson was tired of his damn ears throbbing. He'd been stuck in this goddamn truck in back of the old lady's place for over a month with this idiot Angel. He should have ridden with Byron, he thought.

"Who you orderin' around, Fool?" Angel turned in his seat to face him.

"We'll see who the fool is when Moon can't get us on the goddamn phone 'cause we can't fuckin' hear it!" He spoke without losing eye contact with Griffin.

"Put the fuckin' thing on vibrate!" Angel yelled.

"The whole fuckin' truck is vibrating, bitch! How'm I supposed to feel the goddamn phone?"

"Hey, I don't have a fuckin' problem hearing my phone, asshole. Turn up the goddamn volume!" Angel cranked the sound up higher still in protest.

"Turn it down!" Jerome screamed.

"Fuck you!" Angel screamed back.

The decibel level was at eardrum-bursting level now. They would never hear a phone call over that. They couldn't even hear themselves screaming. How could they possibly hear the sirens of the fire truck that was speeding toward them?

~

Moon waited impatiently in the hallway. What the hell was the old lady doing?

"Hey!" he called. "What the hell you doin' in there?" There was no response.

He couldn't hear any movement. He reached down and unhooked the leash and muzzle from the dog's collar.

"Sic 'em," he hissed. The dog ran to the doorway, Moon beside him. Moon kicked the door wide open, as hard as he could. If the old lady had a gun she would have to shoot the dog first. The dog entered the room snarling and barking. Moon came in a second later. It was empty, totally empty.

"Mother fucker!" Moon yelled. The dog was still snarling and barking. Moon looked in the direction of whatever had the dog's attention. Staring back through the un-curtained streaked window was Georgia. Arms folded, she stood defiantly on the fire escape, smiling. Moon rushed to the window. He tried to open it; it wouldn't budge. The dog stopped barking now. A low growl replaced the previous sound. Moon looked down. The dog was staring at him.

"Shut the fuck up!" he ordered. The dog's stare continued, unfaltering. The growling continued. It became louder, almost in stereo. He spun around. There in the doorway were two more pit bulls. He recognized them immediately. 'Motherfucker!" he said under his breath. He reached slowly into his overcoat pocket.

Georgia smiled as the dogs attacked. She wouldn't watch too long, she told herself. That would make her a monster, like him. She would watch long enough to be sure he wasn't going to survive the attack. Long enough to know that he had endured the same agonizing death he had bestowed upon her daughter. Georgia smiled as the tears ran down her face.

~

AJ frantically dialed Moon's number again. Why didn't he answer? There had been a terrible accident in the parking lot. A fire truck had just annihilated Angel's truck. What were the odds? The truck that had caused the Hummer to burst into flames was now putting out the blaze. Byron wasn't answering either. That wasn't like him. He was Moon's right hand man, Mr. Efficiency. What the hell was going on? He dialed again, a new number this time. Delia's voice came as a relief.

"Hey, Baby," she breathed.

"Something's wrong here!" he gasped. "I don't know what the fuck to do. Angel and Jerome just got creamed, man!"

"What? What do you mean?"

"A fire truck man! It just hit them head on. The whole damn truck's burning up! They didn't get out!" There was a distinct air of panic in his voice. "Nobody's answering their phones! I can't get hold of your brother!"

"Are the police there yet?" she asked earnestly.

"Not yet."

"Get out of there!" she ordered.

"What about your brother?"

"Fuck him!" She spat into the phone.

AJ steered his car out of the parking lot as the first police cars arrived on the scene. Moon was going to kill him. As if it wasn't reason enough that had AJ been living with Moon's sister while he had been inside, now he had left Moon without a ride and police all over the place. AJ shook his head. Moon was still on probation. This could be bad if he was found in the old woman's apartment, especially with the girl. Moon was going to be pissed off. AJ didn't look forward to seeing him tomorrow.

Chapter Eighteen

Jim exited the cove and walked toward the shore. He could see Margo sitting at the end of the wooden jetty. His jetty, he thought. He had had it built so he could take the boat back and forth from their slip in Carmel during the summer months. Cassi had loved the boat. She was a good sailor, too. Sailing was the one real passion she and Jim had shared. When they were on the water she was a complete daddy's girl. Shame, she had not stepped foot on the boat since Jim had left. He sighed heavily.

His footsteps on the wood alerted Margo to his presence. She turned, nodded her acknowledgement casually, and returned her attention to a cup of coffee she was cradling in both hands. Jim stopped about five feet short of the end of the jetty. He stood there awkwardly, his hands in his pockets.

"Hey," he called.

"Hey," Margo replied. She placed the cup down beside her and turned to face him, her legs dangling softly over the edge of the wood. She put her hand down behind her for support. "What's up?"

"Carla said you were down here."

"Yes I am," Margo confirmed.

"I … I … uhh, stopped by to pick up the boxes. Carla said you didn't fill them yet." He moved his foot as if putting out an imaginary cigarette.

"Not yet," Margo replied shrugging. "I'll do it."

"When?" he asked. "I was supposed to give the clothing to the shelter, remember?"

"I forgot," she said flatly. "I'll get around to it."

"If you want, Carla and I can …"

"I'll do it," she said sternly.

"Margo, it's time to let go. You have to …"

"I said I'll do it!" she snapped. "I'm not ready yet." She turned back to her original position, ignoring him.

"Okay." They both stared out at the ocean for what seemed an eternity. The silence was uncomfortable to say the least.

"So, did you have someone check the supports yet?" he asked.

"What?" Margo inquired, confused. She turned back around to face him.

"The wooden supports for the dock," he replied. "They have to be checked for rot. I told you, remember?"

"I forgot," Margo said with a sigh. "I need to get someone to look at them. They haven't been touched since you left."

"I never left, Margo," Jim said with a small laugh in his throat. "You kicked me out." He looked to see a smile spread across her face.

"Yes, I did, didn't I?" She raised her chin and one eyebrow defiantly. "That was a pretty good fight."

"Yes, it was," he said rubbing his chin. "You had one hell of a left."

"I still do," she said menacingly.

"Maybe it's a good thing that I'm getting out of town for a while then," he said crouching into a squat. He focused on a small rock laying on the wood. He picked it up and began to trace the grain of the wood with it. He looked sideways at Margo. She was not making eye contact. "I'm thinking of trying France out for a while," he said.

"You're thinking of trying it out?" she asked. "What does that mean?"

"Well, I've got a couple of movies I want to work on over there. Maybe I'll come back when they're done, maybe not. I'll have to see how it goes."

"When does all this happen?" She tried not to sound too interested.

"That depends," he said looking up at her. He held his stare until she turned her face away.

"On what?" Margo picked at some imaginary lint on her capris.

"I'm trying to figure out if there's anything worth staying here for." He rolled the pebble around in his fingers. "Can you think of anything that might be worth me staying for, Margo?" His eyes never strayed from her face.

"Not off the top of my head. No," she replied coolly.

"That's a shame," he said, rising. He threw the pebble far out into the ocean, turned silently, and began his walk back to the house.

Margo opened her mouth to call him back, but thought better of it, and let him go. She watched him until he vanished from view inside the cove. She shook her head, scolding herself. "Stupid, stupid, stupid."

Chapter Nineteen

"You don't have to do this, Margo. It's too much," Carla complained. "She's only five weeks pregnant."

"Hey, you only have a first grandchild once," Margo countered. "I know Lisa will be relieved to have you there." Margo shuffled Carla toward the gate.

"I could have driven, Margo. You didn't have to fly me up there." Carla didn't sound as appreciative as Margo had hoped. "And for two months? Paid in advance? Are you sure everything's alright? Are you trying to get rid of me?"

"Don't be ridiculous, Carla," Margo snapped. "I'm sorry if I got a little over zealous, but I'm never going to be a grandmother. I just thought that this was the time you should be with your only daughter, when she needs you. You never know if you'll get another chance."

"Oh, Margo, I'm sorry. I didn't think …." Carla stopped walking and turned to face her boss. Her face contorted with guilt, which was exactly what Margo had intended. "I didn't mean …"

"That's okay, darling," Margo cooed. "Now come on," she said pushing again, "you're going to miss that flight."

Margo watched as Carla placed her shoes and jacket into an open plastic bin and pushed them along with her bag onto the conveyor. She handed the airport security her ticket and driver's license. When he was completely assured, without a doubt, that the red-haired, freckle-faced, middle-aged, overweight woman was not an Iraqi terrorist, he waved her through into the terminal. Carla retrieved her belongings on the other side of the checkpoint and slipped on her shoes. She waved her ticket in the air, and Margo cheerily waved back. Then Carla vanished from sight. Margo casually flipped open her phone and hit the redial. Someone picked up. "She's gone," she said softly.

Margo had not seen Peta or anyone from the group since that Friday, the night of 'the event.' The Fourth of July celebrations had passed uneventfully for Margo on Wednesday. She and Carla had spent the evening playing Boggle, eating pizza, and drinking beer. At about eight o'clock Lisa had called with the news of her pregnancy. By eight forty-five Margo had hatched the plan to get her out of the house. By nine o'clock she had purchased Carla's ten a.m. ticket to San Francisco.

The group leader, or Audrey, as Margo now knew her, had gone to Seattle after the last meeting, giving everyone the week off. So the comrades in arms had not had a chance to discuss the events of last week. Now, with Carla out of the way, Margo could have them all over to her house. This place was like Fort Knox. They had total privacy.

Margo surveyed the set-up in the kitchen. Not bad, considering this had been thrown together in just a few short hours. Granted, she had not really done anything. There were four large chafing dishes filled with various offerings from Valentino's restaurant in town. There was an assortment of soft drinks and wine. After Peta's comment on her last brewing attempt, she felt a little inadequate as a barista and had picked up coffee from Starbucks. On the table also sat an array of desserts. It looked more like a cocktail party than a ... er ... Margo wasn't sure what this was.

The security box from the gate buzzed. Margo pushed a small button on the wall receiver. "Hello?"

"Hey, Margo; it's Doug." His voice crackled on the system. "I have Peta and Georgia with me."

"Hi guys!" Margo pushed a second button to open the gate. This was weird. It felt almost like family coming to visit. She smiled to herself. She hadn't felt like she had family in a long time. Before Doug had even reached the front of the house the buzzer sounded again.

"Hello, it's Melody and Raul," Melody's cheerful voice came over the intercom.

"Oh. Er ... Hi. Come on in, guys." Margo felt awkward as she pushed the button. Why was Raul here? Did he know about the events of last week? How many people knew? Margo felt a sudden twinge of panic.

"Moses and Bernadette are right behind us," Melody chirped.

"Okay." Margo tried to sound calm. She knew Bernadette, Moses' wife, from last week. They were an awesome, but somewhat odd-looking couple. Bernadette was a five-foot-three Jewish-Italian girl from Brooklyn, while Moses measured in at six-foot-four, and was probably the blackest black man Margo had ever met. He had a laid back, cool, west coast air about him, while Bernadette spoke loudly, firing her words rapidly, and incessantly waved her arms. Margo was looking forward to seeing them together. She liked diversity in all things. She walked over to the front door and flung it open ready to greet her guests, just in time to see Doug's car pull up in front.

The group ate first, casually, nonchalantly. The conversation was light, without mention of the previous week. Margo was the perfect host. She made sure everyone had enough to eat and that their glasses were full. By the time dessert and coffee came around she was a little tired, not to mention tipsy from her three glasses of wine. The group drifted outside to the deck overlooking the ocean.

"Okay, guys, there are a few things we need to discuss. I want to make sure we are all on the same page here." Doug sounded very authoritarian. "Just to put everyone's mind at rest, my sources tell me that absolutely no usable evidence was found by police at the scene last Friday. That's good. We all wore our gloves and hairnets; great job. As you know from Saturday's paper, they found the two gunshot victims," he shot a side glance at Moses, "and what was left of Haines in the apartment next to Georgia's. They have tied the two to a drug deal gone wrong. That's awesome; nothing to link anybody to any of us." Georgia breathed out audibly. "As for the two in the Hummer, they got a two-inch write-up in the paper about the accident with the fire truck, with them having a suspected connection to the drug deal that was going down."

"Well, I personally would like to say a big thank you to everyone here." Georgia rose and bowed her gratitude to the other members of the group. "I was scared to death, but knowing you were all right there helped me to be brave. You people have set me and my granddaughter free. Melody, without you orchestrating all this from your dispatch position, I don't know if we could have timed it quite as perfectly. So, thank you for letting us know Moon's whereabouts, and for sending the fire truck when you did."

"Oh, you need to thank some friends in the LAPD for keeping track of Moon," Melody said smiling. "As for the fire truck, I will take credit for that. I had to make sure all calls for a fire truck went elsewhere. That particular firehouse only has one truck. I had to make sure they were the ones to answer the call. We had a little help from a couple of other dispatchers there, too."

"So why did the fire engine show up, Doug?" Margo asked innocently.

"They were actually answering a call about a fire in one of the empty apartments. It was probably lit by homeless people." Doug cleared his throat.

"In July?" Margo asked innocently.

"Yes, Margo, in July. Allow me to introduce you to the homeless person who started the fire." He pointed in Raul's direction. Raul stood up and took a small bow.

"Oh, so it wasn't really an accident?" Margo was genuinely surprised. "I wondered how a Hummer could just burst into flames like that."

"It had a little help, Margo." Doug shook his head.

"So, the firefighters were in on this?" Margo persisted.

"Jesus, Margo! What is this, twenty questions?" Doug was getting irritated.

"Excuse me, Doug! I know the roles we all played in this. I just didn't know we were getting as much help from the outside, that's all. I thought the fewer people that were involved the better it was." Margo wasn't about to let Doug bully her.

"You're absolutely right, Margo," Doug said apologetically. "I actually invited a couple of these guys to help if they wanted to. They had a history with this gang."

"How's that?" Raul asked.

"About three years ago," Doug recited, "there was a drive-by shooting involving one of Haines' guys. He was left for dead on the sidewalk. A fire truck was dispatched with two paramedics on board."

"Oh, I remember that!" Georgia interrupted. "Haines' gang arrived on the scene and started shooting at a couple of bystanders who they thought did it, right?"

"Right," Doug attested. "Both paramedics died from gunshot wounds, one at the scene and the other at the hospital."

"So this was payback," Margo said in realization.

"Something like that," Doug answered without emotion.

"That's freakin' awesome, man!" Raul smiled radiantly. "We took five pieces of shit off the street!"

"What about the dogs?" Melody asked, openly concerned.

"We got a call Friday night from a concerned neighbor," Bernadette began.

"That was me!" Georgia interrupted.

"When we got there Moon, or Haines, whatever you want to call him was in little pieces all over the place." Bernadette hung her head. "The dogs had to be destroyed."

"Well, that doesn't seem right," Melody protested. "Those poor dogs."

"Those poor dogs were trained killers," Bernadette added, holding up her hands. "There was no way of getting the fighter out of them. They'd tasted too much blood, long before last week. The one good thing is that they died for a good cause."

"A good cause," Margo said. "Is that what we're calling it?"

"You bet your ass that's what we're calling it," Doug said loudly and defiantly. "You thought this was a good cause a week and-a-half ago. Don't change your mind now. We're all in this together. Right?"

"Absolutely!" Margo said standing. She held up her wine glass. "The Support Group!" she said proudly.

"The Support Group!" echoed the others.

"Oh, wait, wait!" Melody rose from her seat. She walked quickly inside and returned a few moments later with two cardboard boxes that measured roughly two-by-eight inches. "The Solomons asked me to bring these. They couldn't make it."

"The Solomons?" Margo whined. "How did they know? Who told them?"

"I did," Melody said sheepishly. "Lena called me the day after we went to the bar. She knew we were planning something. She was sad because she and Art are too old to be of any use. She said that if they can be of any help in the future to just let them know."

"In the future?" asked Doug.

Margo took one of the boxes from Melody. She opened it and found it to be full of business cards. She took a few out and passed them around. The cards were a matt black with a small embossed silver set of scales in the center. On each dish of the scale, perfectly balanced sat a silver eye, like the Egyptian eye of Anubis. Below the scale was a banner on which the words 'Do Unto Others' were imprinted.

"The scales of justice," Moses declared. He nodded toward Doug.

"An eye for an eye," Margo whispered.

"Do Unto Others?" Peta questioned. "What kind of business card is that?"

"That's not a business card," Doug said. "It's a calling card."

Chapter Twenty

Margo walked slowly back and forth across the width of the large fireplace, surveying the many framed photographs. The Solomon kids were a good-looking bunch. The girls were both pretty, but with noses that were slightly too big for their delicate faces. Art's genes in action, Margo noted. The same noses, however, seemed to fit perfectly on their brothers; how chauvinistic, Margo thought. All four had dark brown eyes and hair, full red lips, and perfect teeth. Margo picked up a graduation photo of what appeared to be the youngest son.

"That's my Aaron," Lena Solomon said proudly. "His smile could melt you."

"He certainly was a good-looking boy," Margo agreed. She replaced the frame carefully and picked up the one next to it. "Is this Aaron, too?"

"No, that's his brother David. They were eight years apart. They didn't really even get to know each other very well. David was the eldest; Aaron was the baby." Margo noted how both were spoken of in the past tense.

"David wasn't around while Aaron was growing up?" Margo was surprised. The family pictures depicted a close bond between the siblings.

"David joined the Marine Corp after 9-1-1. He was nineteen; Aaron was only eleven when he left. He came home on leave three times during his four years of service. Each time he was a little more distant. When he got out he didn't come home. He was running with a pretty bad crowd up in Oakland. He managed to land himself in prison on a drug trafficking charge back in 2005. He got six years, but only served two. Art was devastated. He didn't handle it very well at all. He disowned him."

She smiled warmly at Margo and Peta. "Aagh! Jewish men! So dramatic! Aaron died while David was in prison. It seems David couldn't forgive himself for not being here, and Art couldn't forgive him for not being here either. When David got out of prison he vanished. So I lost both my sons! Funny, how one bullet could kill six people. It destroyed my whole family."

"You haven't spoken to him since?" Peta thought that was the saddest story she had ever heard.

"He calls sometimes on my birthday. He doesn't say much. Just, 'I love you, Mama.' He doesn't tell me where he is or what he's doing, and I don't ask. I just tell him I love him, too." She sighed heavily. "He gave me a post office box to send mail to if I should need to contact him. I've sent him a few things, but he hasn't replied so I don't know if he got them. It's my birthday in September. Maybe he'll call." She shrugged.

Margo could feel Lena Solomon's sorrow. It was in the very air around them. It was reflected through her eyes and evident in her forced smile. It was displayed in the multitude of family photos. This was a broken woman. But there was something more, something that was weighing heavily on her.

"Why did you ask us here today, Lena?" Margo tried to sound as comforting as she could. "What is it you need from us?"

"Please come into the office." She gestured toward the rear of the house. "My Aaron was a computer wizard," she said proudly. "He hooked up all the surveillance cameras at the store to this computer. He would brag how close up he could get with the digital cameras he had bought. Come, I'll show you."

They entered a large office, furnished with heavy, rich-looking mahogany furniture and red leather. The scent of pipe tobacco clung to the furnishings. It reminded Margo of Jim's man cave. On top of the desk sat a computer monitor, one of the larger, older ones. Lena walked around the desk and fired up the computer. It was quite fast for an older model. Lena went into the documents file and clicked on the 'my videos' folder. There she clicked on a folder entitled, July 15 2007. The Windows Media Player kicked into play. Margo gave a small gasp. There was Aaron Solomon behind the counter of his parents' jewelry store. He was polishing the jewelry. Two men entered the store. Margo realized immediately that this was the actual footage of Aaron's death. She placed her hand over her mouth. The men said something to Aaron, and the man on the left drew a gun from his pocket. He aimed it at Aaron's head. Aaron quickly started to pull the trays of jewelry from inside the showcase.

Lena hit the pause button. She clicked on the still picture and a tiny magnifying glass with a plus sign in the center appeared. Lena kept clicking and the picture got bigger and clearer. She zoomed in on the man's left hand. The gun looked huge now; his finger clearly visible on the trigger. She kept clicking. She zoomed in on the man's pinkie finger — to a gold ring engraved with a clenched fist, the pinky and index finger extended. Lena hit the print button.

"Mal Occhio," Peta whispered, "to ward off the evil eye. I've never seen it on a ring before. On a chain around the neck, yes."

"Neither had we, and we're jewelers." Lena exited from the picture much to Margo's satisfaction. She was horrified that she might have to watch the actual shooting. "Here is another video shot three months later." Again the video showed two men entering the store. This time they spoke with Art. No guns were drawn, but the man on the left placed both his hands palm down on the case while he leaned forward to speak. Again Lena did her magic with the zoom button. The man wore an identical ring on his pinky, as the shooter in the robbery. Again, Lena hit the print button.

"We don't have audio, but he was telling my husband that he would be back the following Friday and every Friday thereafter for an envelope containing $5,000. This was to ensure our safety in the community, he said. We didn't realize that this was the same guy who killed my Aaron until we played the tape back and saw the ring." Lena exited again; this time her hands were shaking. "There's one more," she said in a low voice. Lena pressed the play button and the last video jumped to life. Again the two men entered the store. This time Art acted as though he was reaching for the money to give them. Instead he came from under the counter with a hand gun. He aimed the gun at the man wearing the ring and fired. The gun apparently jammed. He tried to shoot again. By this time the other man, much larger in stature, jumped the counter and was suddenly beside Art, beating him mercilessly. Art fell to the floor, where he was continuously kicked violently. The attacker then raised a foot and stamped down hard with his heel. He repeated the action, and then returned to the kicking motion. Margo felt sick, even though most of the violence was hidden behind the counter. "He broke both of Art's shins," Lena said without emotion. The man with the ring then leaned over the counter, apparently saying something to Art. He spat on Art, and then both men turned and left. "He was telling

Art that if there wasn't $15,000 waiting for them the following Monday, he would be burying his daughters in pieces. If he told anyone, he would be signing his daughters' death warrant. We paid them the $15,000, and we've been paying them $5,000 every Friday since, rain or shine."

"Oh, my God, Lena; this is awful!" Peta sounded distraught.

"That's why I called you. They told us a couple of weeks ago that they wanted more. They said they want $10,000 a week. We told them we don't have that kind of money. We've already used up our savings. Sales are down; the store's going under. We have nowhere else to turn. We hoped you could help." Lena's face looked suddenly hopeful.

"Lena," Margo began, "what exactly do you think we can do?"

"Well, you helped Georgia. I thought the group could do the same for us." Her eyes pleaded with the two women.

"That was different." Margo racked her brain for excuses.

"How was it different? You said at the meeting, 'How long are we going to be victims? How long are we going to take this shit?' I thought you meant it."

"I did, but Lena, these guys are hoods. This looks like organized crime." Margo shook her head. "We can't go up against these guys."

"No, no, you're wrong. It's just these two. They're not connected to anyone, I'm positive." Lena put her hands together in the praying position.

"Lena, for God's sake, I'm an actress! Peta's a dance instructor!"

"Actually, I'm a choreographer," Peta interjected.

Margo shot Peta an icy glare. "Lena, we're not guns for hire. We're just ordinary people. This is out of our …"

"You have to help us! They've got my daughter!" Lena collapsed into tears.

"Jesus Christ!" Margo said shaking her head. "When the hell did we turn into the Magnificent Seven?"

Chapter Twenty-One

"Absolutely not!" Doug's face was purple. "What the hell is wrong with you people?"

"I didn't say we'd do it!" Margo protested. "I just told her I'd mention it to you guys."

"With a view to what Margo?" Doug held up his hands in despair. "On the off chance that we might all be up for whacking a couple of hoods?"

"I never …"

"You never what, Margo? Let me tell you something." He strode across the deck holding his pointed index finger two inches from her forehead. "You!" he snarled, "are not Angie Dickinson." He spun quickly pointing at Peta. "She is not Wonder Woman, I'm not Petrocelli, and he," he said pointing at Moses, "is not fucking Shaft!"

"But I *could* be Shaft," Moses suggested. He took a swig from his Corona bottle.

"I'll be Foxy Brown," Melody said, bobbing her head and clicking her fingers.

"I ought to slap you both!" Georgia snapped. "Those were the worst movies ever made. Now Sidney Poitier, in In the Heat of the Night, *that* was a good movie."

"Can we get back to the point here?" Doug raised his eyebrows. "We are not a hit squad, or a vigilante group. We can't just meter out justice whenever we …"

"Why not?" Moses asked. The rest of the group looked at him. "Why not?" he repeated.

"We can't just … Come on! … What the hell can we …" Doug was searching his brain for answers and the rest of the group for support with his eyes.

"I spent twenty-three years dealing with pieces of shit like these on the street, every day. They don't go away, even after you put 'em away. They keep coming back. The courts let 'em out rehabilitated; huh! There is no justice. I watched my partner of eighteen years bleed to death in my arms. My blood and his, mixed together on the sidewalk. 'Blood brothers in death.' He was shot by a rehabilitated parolee, on the outside for a week and-a-half. I killed the guy who pulled the trigger, but not the one who pulled the strings."

Moses walked across the deck to a large copper ice chest. He helped himself to another Corona. No one said a word, waiting for the rest of whatever he had to say. He popped the top and took a swig. "The ones who really killed my best friend and made me a cripple never paid. They just kept on dealing their drugs, making their deals, messing up other peoples' lives. We all knew who they were, but we couldn't touch 'em. We needed proof, evidence, witnesses. We needed justice. But the judicial system doesn't work. I used to think it did, but now I know better. So we never got our justice. Victims *never* get justice. So why not make our own?"

"Can you hear yourself?" Doug stared earnestly into Moses' eyes. "We can't just take the law into our own hands!"

"Why not?"

"Would you stop fucking saying that!"

"I know people — lots of people — on both sides of the law, who feel the same way." Moses waved his bottle around the room. "Look at the contacts we have right here. Hell! Look at what we just did!"

"Are you fucking serious? Do you have any idea how much money it takes to organize shit like that?" Doug waved Moses off.

"I have money," Margo interrupted.

"Shut up, Margo," Doug ordered.

"I'm serious," she persisted.

"Margo, shut up!" Doug said firmly.

"No. No. Listen! I'm extremely wealthy!" She exclaimed excitedly.

"Margo! You're not fucking helping here!"

Margo turned her attention to Moses. "I was paid six million for my last movie," she said flatly. "Five million for the one before that, and seven …"

"Hey!" Moses yelled, beaming. "We got a sponsor!"

"Moses! Get a fucking grip!" Doug pleaded. "We can't do this."

"We got the police department right here," Moses said, slapping his chest hard.

"We've got 9-1-1, too!" Melody stood up.

"Hey man! I got your back in the Big House!" Raul rose, grinning.

"This is crazy!" Doug said. "You're all fuckin' nuts!"

"I think we may have the fire department," Moses teased.

Doug broke into a smile, shaking his head in disbelief. "You're crazy, man!"

"And hey!" Moses gestured in Margo's direction. "We've even got Hollywood!"

Chapter Twenty-Two

Sal Cicci yanked Ruth out of the car violently. "Remember what I said," he snapped. "I have no problem taking the old man out. You'd better do as you're told." He watched as his buddy Paulie Venetto, emerged from inside the car. "You got your friend?" Sal asked.

"Not yet," Paulie grinned. He reached back into the car for a rather beat-up looking baseball bat. He carefully opened his long raincoat. He slipped one hand through a large hole in the pocket and gripped the middle of the bat so that when he closed the coat it was totally obscured from view. It was also readily available to become a lethal weapon when the time was right. Not as efficient as the .38 in the waistband of his pants, but much more intimidating, and certainly more enjoyable to use. "Now I do."

"If it comes to it, fuck the bat and use the gun," Sal admonished.

"Hey!" Paulie answered defiantly. "Do I tell you how to handle yourself?"

"No," Sal answered. "But we've gotta be careful. This could be a setup. You do what you gotta do."

"What setup?" Paulie laughed. "He's not going to pull anything while we've got his kid."

The three of them walked toward the large, corrugated iron building. Paulie slid the tall door open. Sal looked around. He saw a pair of dirty sneakers without laces sticking out from inside a large shipping crate close by. He kicked one of them hard. A dirty-looking man in torn clothing and an oily knit hat rolled out of it, an empty bottle in his hand.

"You," Sal snapped. "Get the fuck outa here. Now!"

The disheveled man rose and staggered off, disoriented. "Fucking bums," Sal muttered.

They entered the warehouse. Sal pulled a pair of handcuffs from his pocket. He attached one end to Ruth's wrist. He looked around for something to fasten the other end to.

"You're going leave me here?" Ruth was almost hysterical.

"Don't worry, we'll tell Daddy where to find you," Sal said with a snarl in his voice. He fastened the other end to an old forklift in the middle of the floor.

"This place is full of homeless people and drug addicts," Ruth said. "You can't leave me here!"

"If you shut your mouth they won't know you're in here," he smiled. "And if they do come in, just be hospitable." The two men laughed mockingly, in unison. Ruth watched in horror as the two men exited and pulled the huge door back into the closed position, leaving her paralyzed with fear in the dark.

Sal and Paulie got back into the car and drove slowly away. The wharf was once again silent. Silent, but for the sound of sneakers on gravel. The dirty-looking man in the oily knit hat, crept slowly around the side of the building toward the warehouse door. He looked around cautiously and quietly slid the heavy door open. He looked around again, before stepping inside and pulling the door closed behind him.

~

This was the big one. Sal could feel it. They would be able to return to New York after this one. They would be able to get Bonasera off their backs for good. No more looking over their shoulders. No more peering through blinds before answering the door. He eyed the briefcase by Paulie's feet — two hundred and fifty-thousand — soon to be worth well over a million in uncut diamonds. They would use half of that to pay Bonasera his money plus vig, and more. He would be satisfied with that; Sal was sure of it. That was more than enough to call off a hit. With the rest they could set up their own racket. Maybe Bonasera would let them work the Jersey shore again. They would soon be free.

The old man better be right about this. If not, the deal was off, and they would stay here, and he would keep paying. They were to meet at warehouse twenty-three at one o'clock. Solomon had a jeweler friend who owed him. The jeweler had agreed to part with some hot stones for the same price she had paid for them. Solomon had assured him of their value. It didn't matter; Sal had a friend waiting to appraise them. Solomon wasn't getting the girl back until Sal knew what he had … if Solomon got the girl back. Depending on how things turned out, Sal and Paulie could well end up with the diamonds and the money. The jeweler had a bodyguard. She needed one. Sal would have to access the situation at the warehouse, to see what could be done. Over a million in diamonds was a score, but over a million in diamonds and two-hundred and fifty-thousand in cash was better.

The overcast sky of the Los Angeles morning was behind them. The sun was hot, sitting high in an ocean of blue. Paulie pulled his raincoat conspicuously closed. He stood motionless, waiting for Sal to join him. Sal had been like a big brother to him. He was the only one who had ever talked nice to Paulie. He was the only one who called him Paulie. Mr. Bonasera always called him 'meathead. Mr. Bonasera always told him to dummy up. Paulie didn't want to go back to New York. They had it good here. Nobody knew who they were here. They could start their own business, one where Paulie didn't have to hit people all the time. Paulie liked hitting people, but not all the time. He didn't like hitting women and old men, but if Sal said it was necessary, then he would do it. He would do it for Sal. He would move back to New York for Sal. Sal would take care of him.

"You got your friend?" Sal asked.

"He's right here.," Paulie answered grinning, patting the left side of his coat.

They marched purposefully toward the door marked twenty-three. Sal swung the briefcase, his arms almost robotic. Paulie walked swiftly but stiffly because of his wooden appendage.

The door stood slightly open. Paulie violently slid it wider. Inside it was brightly lit from an opening in the roof that allowed cargo to be lowered directly into the building by crane. At a small, folding table sat a woman. She was an attractive redhead. Her hair was pulled back tightly in a bun, and she wore horn-rimmed glasses. There was something vaguely familiar about her, Sal thought. She was too hot-looking to be a jeweler. Before her on the table was a small pull-string leather pouch. Behind her stood a tall black man. Taller than Paulie by an inch or two, Sal surmised, but nowhere near as powerful. Paulie could take him. To her right and their left was Solomon. He annoyed Sal. Weakness always annoyed Sal. A cell phone rang.

"Excuse me, gentlemen; I need to take this." Margo pulled a phone from her pocket.

"What the fuck?" Sal protested.

"I might be able to get more stones. If you're interested?" Margo countered. She knew Sal's greed would give her permission.

"We're interested. Put it on speaker." Sal nodded his approval. Margo flipped open the phone.

"Were you successful?" she said into the air.

"Yes, I have the goods," Raul's voice came over the speaker.

"Can we proceed?" Margo asked.

Raul pulled the oily knit hat from his head. He smiled across the car at Ruth. "Go right ahead."

Deftly, Moses drew the gun from the back of his waistband. Almost instantaneously, a shot was heard and Sal fell to his knees. A red circle neatly positioned in the center of his forehead.

"Sal!" Paulie's pain was evident. He drew the bat from his coat and raised it above his head menacingly. Moses pointed the gun at his face and Paulie halted.

"No!" Margo shouted. "Do unto others, remember? Don't shoot him!"

The door slid open behind Paulie. He turned. There stood a middle-aged, overweight, Irish man, holding a bat. Paulie smiled. "Are you fucking serious?" he said mockingly.

One after the other, four more men holding bats, entered the building. They were wearing dock workers' attire, but their clean-cut appearance and physical stature implied to Margo that they were more than likely policemen or fire fighters.

"Oh!" Doug replied. "We're fucking serious all right. Margo, get out!"

Chapter Twenty-Three

"Who found 'em?" Rick Sawyer scanned the two bodies before him.

"Night watchman," Joe Sanchez replied. "He's outside if you want to talk to him."

"Yeah, keep him here." He crouched over the bloodiest of the two corpses. "Wow! This guy took a beating." The powdery film that seemed to cover everything and the heavy chalk lines around the bodies told him that the CSI team had already been there. One man stood nearby, still taking photographs of the scene. "Did they find anything?"

"A few prints, but the place was pretty much clean, except for a card that was left. Forensics gave me a photo of it." He dug in his inside pocket and retrieved a Polaroid picture.

Sawyer didn't take the photo from Sanchez's outstretched hand. "They both died here, I think," he said, looking at the wall behind him. "See, there's spattering on the wall from the back of the head. Did they find the slug?"

"Yep! Looks like a 38 caliber," Sanchez said flicking through his notepad. Once again he offered the photograph.

"It looks like they both died about the same time, too. Look at the blood. Neither looks fresher than the other." Sawyer pointed at a spot on the floor where Cicci's and Venetto's blood ran into each other. "Yep. This is definitely where they both bled out." He ignored the outstretched hand again. He was in the zone now. "Did either of them have anything on them?"

"The guy who took the bullet is Sal Cicci. He had his wallet in his pocket with five hundred cash in it. Robbery wasn't a motive here." He again flicked through his notes. "He has quite a rap sheet on the east coast: Served five out of ten for armed robbery in ninety-three, got out in the summer of ninety-eight; Was linked to the Bonasera crime family, in New York; Not a made man, but definitely a wannabe; Was apparently running a numbers racket in New Jersey up until 2005, when he vanished from the radar. Rumor has it he owed Bonasera money and had to get out of Dodge. The big guy had no ID and less than twenty dollars on him. We believe his name is Paulie Venetto, but right now the face doesn't match the picture we have on file. He was a bruiser for Bonasera in New York, before he was sent to New Jersey to keep an eye on Cicci. Apparently, they both skipped town around the same time." Joe Sanchez slipped his pen into his breast pocket.

"This was a pretty brutal beating," Sawyer said. "Look at the ridge on the top of the head. It looks like he took two blows to the head at the same time, forcing the skull to crush upward. So I think there were at least two assailants, and judging by the size of this guy, probably more." Sanchez smiled. Sawyer should have been in forensics. "But why the beating? They shot the other guy. Why beat this one to death?"

"Maybe they were sending a message," Sanchez offered, shrugging.

"Maybe this was in retaliation," Sawyer surmised. "You said this guy was a bruiser. Did he use a bat?"

"The report didn't say." Sanchez leafed through his notes again. "I'll check on it." He quickly wrote something illegible on a blank page."

"Anything else?" Sawyer said, standing.

"You wanna take a look at this?" Sanchez held out the photo impatiently.

Sawyer perused the picture carefully. "Aw shit!" he muttered.

"What?"

"Is Castillo back from his FMLA yet?" He was clearly aggravated.

"Not until next week.," Sanchez replied. "Why?"

"What about Johannsen?" Sawyer pressed.

"She's still on maternity." Sanchez shrugged.

"Shit!" Sawyer spat. "I'm going to Maui next month. I can't take this case. My wife will kill me!"

"What's the big deal?" Sanchez said shrugging again. "Just fill out the report, and do what you can before you go."

"Look at the card. We've got scales, an eye for an eye, and do unto others. This is a vigilante group," Sawyer declared.

"So what? It doesn't mean there's going to be another one. This could have been the only target they had."

"You don't print up cards like these one at a time. Somebody's got a box full." Sawyer waved the photo in the air. "I've got a feeling these are going to be turning up all over L.A. Shit!"

Chapter Twenty-Four

Arthur Lewis followed the arrows. A sign read "Level 6"; he was close now. He could feel the excitement welling up inside. *Stay calm,* he told himself. He didn't want this Rodriguez guy to think he was too eager. Then the price would go up. Five grand was a good price, he thought. He'd paid more in the past, but not for a twelve-year-old. And he got to keep this one. His palms were sweating as he clutched the steering wheel tighter. Level 7.

The sun was already bright in the sky as he emerged from the inner parking garage onto the eighth floor, roof level. He squinted as he scoped the area for his prey. There in the outer corner of the roof lot was parked a tan 1979 Chevy van. A Hispanic man was leaned up against it, arms folded. Lewis aimed the car in that direction. He pulled up alongside the van and rolled down his window.

"Rodriguez?" Lewis asked nervously.

"Yeah," Raul lied. "You Lewis?"

Lewis parked the car and got out. He held out his hand; Raul ignored it. Lewis couldn't possibly know how much the very thought of him made Raul's skin crawl. There was no way he was going to shake his hand.

"Anyone follow you here?" Raul already knew the answer to that one. How many pedophiles involve friends and family, or a police escort, when they're out on the prowl?

"No, no. I made sure nobody knows I'm here. Where is she?" He looked both nervous and excited. Raul watched with disgust as he licked his lips.

"She's in the van," Raul answered curtly. "Where's the money?"

"Oh. It's right here." Lewis pulled an envelope from his inside jacket pocket. "You want to count it?"

"That won't be necessary." Raul was fighting hard to keep the disgust from his voice as he accepted the payment. This piece of shit was buying a little girl. God knows what his intentions were. He'd like to beat the living crap out of him right now, but he had to stick

90

to the plan. *Stick to the script.* Raul walked around to the back of the van, closely followed by Lewis. He pulled open the back doors. Inside was a tall black man, and a slender red-haired woman, bound at the wrists and feet, her mouth covered with tape.

"What's this?" Lewis asked excitedly. "You said she was twelve!"

"There was a problem," Raul said calmly. "I didn't want to come empty-handed. I can give you a break on the price."

"I don't know." Lewis was agitated. "This isn't what we agreed. She's way too old."

Moses jumped down from the back of the van. Lewis stepped back. He lifted the woman from the van and stood her beside them. "Look," Moses said unfastening the rope on Margo's ankles. "This one's older, but she's in good condition. Her ass is real tight," he said, running his hand over her butt. Margo jumped back in apparent horror, but Moses held tight to her bound wrists and pulled her back. "You can do whatever you want to this one. She's an illegal immigrant from Russia; she won't be missed."

"No, she's too old. I don't like them out of their teens." Lewis shook his head. "Give me my money back!"

Moses yanked on the rope that secured Margo's wrists. It came away easily in his hand. Margo reached up and pulled the tape quickly from her mouth. "You sick fuck!" She spat. "You thought I was twelve?"

"Who are you people? Are you police?" Lewis was shaking.

"You've gotten worse," Margo growled. "Now you don't want them out of their teens? You've changed your tune since Houston."

"Who are you?" The color had drained from Lewis' face.

"How old was Melanie Warren? Oh, that's right; she was twenty." Margo took a step toward him.

"Melanie who?" Lewis stepped back; he looked puzzled.

"Melanie Warren!" Margo said loudly. "The one you raped and beat up in your chemistry lab. The one who threw herself out of an eighth floor dorm window." Margo took another step forward, forcing him back against the edge of the roof.

"They never proved that!" Lewis snapped back. "It was consensual."

"You had to say that, didn't you? Your semen was inside her." Margo stepped forward again. Her face was a few inches from his now. "But that didn't explain the bruises that she already had on her body, the ones that weren't a result of the fall."

"The school fired me because of that. I've paid my dues!" Lewis looked nervously to his left, where Raul stood, his face stern. On his right he was flanked by Moses, who smiled casually.

"You paid your dues? You got away with murder, you son of a bitch!" Margo reached behind her and pulled a sheet of paper from inside her waistband. It was a photocopy of a hand-written letter. "Doctor Lewis raped me," she read aloud. "I can't tell anyone." She replaced the paper in her waistband.

"That's not true! We were having an affair."

"Having an affair with a college student only gets you fired; rape gets you prison time," Raul said quietly. "That's why you said you were having consensual sex."

"Melanie's best friend, Donna, got a phone call ten minutes before she jumped. Melanie told her that she was failing your class. You offered to stay behind with her so that she could do some extra credit work to bring up her grade. That's when you raped her, you bastard! You told her that if she told anyone, you would paint her as a slut who had offered sex to get better grades." Margo was talking through clenched teeth. "Luckily for you, Donna's testimony was considered hearsay. You were never formally charged with anything."

Simultaneously, Moses and Raul grabbed Lewis' arms. Margo frisked his body violently until she felt his wallet. She took it out carefully, almost as if touching Lewis was painful to her, throwing it behind her into the van. She reached down into her bra, retrieving something wrapped in a tissue. She carefully folded back the soft paper to reveal a matte black business card. She slipped the card into Lewis' jacket pocket, and stuffed the tissue back into her bra.

"What is that?" Lewis screamed.

"That's your one-way ticket to Hell, asshole!" she said, as Moses and Raul heaved Lewis over the waist high wall that ran the perimeter of the roof. A violent thud a few seconds later told them that he had met with the sidewalk.

Moses leaned out over the wall to survey the damage. "Okay, let's go."

Raul quickly jumped behind the wheel of the van, while Moses and Margo slipped in the back, pulling the doors closed behind them. As the van quickly started it's descent from the roof, Margo flipped open her cell phone and dialed, her face set in a stony stare.

"It's done," she said softly.

"Thank you," Audrey whispered.

Chapter Twenty-Five

Sawyer stepped carefully around the bloody mess on the sidewalk that was once Arthur Lewis. These were brand new shoes. A small crowd had gathered. One young man snapped a photograph.

"Hey!" Sawyer shouted to a uniformed officer. "Get that camera from him." The young man put his hands up in the air as if he were being arrested and mumbled something about a fascist regime.

"Okay folks! Nothing to see here! We have all the witnesses we need; thank you." Joe Sanchez and a rather large black officer were herding the people away from the scene. "I wish they'd hurry up and bag this one. I'm tired of doing crowd control."

"When did this happen?" Sawyer asked looking at his watch.

"About forty-five minutes ago."

"So what makes you think he was pushed?" Sawyer raised one eyebrow.

"What makes you think I think he was pushed?" Sanchez smiled.

"Well, if you got me out of bed at eight-thirty on a Sunday morning for a jumper, you better not eat or drink anything I offer you for the next month." He winked playfully.

Sanchez held out a small zip-loc bag. Inside was a black business card with a set of silver scales. "Someone left a present in his jacket pocket."

"Shit. This is way sooner than I expected," Sawyer grumbled. "Who's the vic?"

"His name is Arthur Frank Lewis, fifty-eight, from San Antonio. Moved here from Houston in '04. His driver's license is missing from his wallet, but everything else was still in there, including three hundred cash. Again, robbery not a motive. He has no priors. Works in the chemistry lab of a local pharmaceutical company. Former college professor, bachelor, lived alone. Was apparently of good moral standing in the community. Worked with troubled teens on a regular basis. Looks like a stand-up guy."

"Well, he's not standing now, is he?' Sawyer remarked. "Someone thought he sucked enough to throw him off a roof." He examined the zip-loc bag that held the familiar black business card. "What could a fifty-eight-year-old college professor do to piss someone off enough to throw him off a roof? Something he did that he didn't get punished for. That's what this is all about." He waved the zip-loc bag in the air. "Check to see if he's been under any investigations at any of the schools he's worked."

"Already did. Nothing."

"Or nothing that was ever documented," Sawyer offered. "These colleges have a great knack for brushing shit under the rug. Don't want to put off possible enrollees. Can't lose that government funding." He scrutinized the face of the card, tracing the embossed scales with his thumb through the thin plastic bag. "Do unto others," he whispered. "Call Doreen in public records. Have her do a check on everywhere he ever worked. See if there was ever a jumper, either at the school or in the area." Looking up, he added, "If there was, I'll bet money it was a girl, from the eighth floor."

Chapter Twenty-Six

"I don't understand. What are they for?" Doug sounded a little disgruntled.

"So we can identify each other," Peta answered.

"Yes, but if we can identify each other, so can the police," Doug argued. "And anyway, we know who we are."

"No, we don't," Moses defended. "We've called in quite a few outsiders. Maybe this is a good way to keep track of who's in."

"Maybe this is a good way of knowing who to prosecute." Doug said grouchily.

"I think it's great," Margo said, turning a small gold lapel pin between her fingers. It was in the shape of a small banner with the initials D U O neatly engraved in the center. "You can't be prosecuted for wearing a pin, Doug."

"No, but you can be recognized as being a member of a group or gang. Why don't we just wear a patch on our backs?" Doug wasn't having any of it.

"Ooh, ooh! We could be Margo's Angels!" Margo teased.

"Kiss my ass, Margo!" Doug snapped. Margo laughed.

"This is the only way the Solomons know how to say thank you. We can't just not accept them," Peta justified. "It would crush them."

"Oh, so let's all get twenty-to-life for murder, to make the Solomons feel better." Doug opened a Corona bottle a little too violently. Its contents foamed up and spilled out. "Shit!" He snarled, brushing his pants.

"How many are there?" Peta asked, ignoring Doug's obvious disgust with the whole thing.

"Well," Margo said, sorting the tiny pieces of jewelry with her index fingernail, "there are two dozen gold ones, and a whole shitload of silver ones. I guess the generals get the gold ones. Hey, Doug! You wanna be a general?"

"Kiss my ass, Margo!" He snapped again. Margo laughed.

"So do we give them out when they sign up, or after they've done the deed?" Peta asked.

"After," Doug snapped. "It can be like an initiation. Like getting your gang colors."

"Ignore Grumpy." Margo nodded sideways toward Doug. "We don't always see the people involved after, so it will have to be before …. when they agree to help out."

"How many silver ones are there?" Moses asked. "Can we all take some? I owe a few of those out already."

Margo held up a medium-sized zipper sealed bag. "There has to be over a hundred of them in here. I think we should all take a dozen."

Peta picked up one of the gold pins and read aloud. "Duo." She looked sheepishly at Margo. "Is anyone going to know what it means?"

"They're not supposed to, unless they're in the group," Margo smiled. "If anyone asks, say it's a community group you're in."

"So what does it stand for?"

"Do Unto Others," Margo said.

"No, I mean if someone asks me …. someone outside the group."

"Don't undercook omelets," Doug said smirking.

"Dry us out!" Moses offered. "You can tell them you're in AA."

"Well, I'm going to say I've joined a companionship group. Like a dating agency," Margo said beaming. "Duo, as in pairs."

"Who's going to believe that?" Doug scoffed. "You're Margo Priestly. Like you can't get a frickin' date!"

"There!" Peta said triumphantly, as she pinned it to the underside of her jacket lapel. "Now it won't matter. I'll only show it to people who are associated with the group."

"Give me a break!" Doug retorted. "What is this? Secret Squirrel?"

"We'll think of something," Margo said laughing. "I still think they're a good …" She was cut short by the ringing of the telephone. "Excuse me," she said picking up a cordless phone on the nearby table. "Hello."

"Margo, it's Jim."

"Oh. Hi, Jim. What's going on?"

"Margo," Jim's voice sounded earnest. "They've got him!"

Chapter Twenty-Seven

Simon Fulton had electric blue eyes. He blinked his long black lashes once in a while as he surveyed the courtroom, grinning. His full lips were pulled back in a broad smile exposing a mouth full of perfectly straight white teeth. His raven hair was cut in one of those messy, just-got-out-of-bed styles that Hollywood seemed to favor nowadays. It accentuated his high cheek bones and strong jaw. He was a looker, all right. In fact, Fulton would probably do very well in Hollywood, if he wasn't facing life imprisonment, or death, for a triple homicide.

This was not the face of a killer, Margo thought. This was a face teenage girls pined over. The kind of eyes that could relieve any young girl of her virginity without pressure. A smile that could convince any mother that her daughter was perfectly safe in his company. The statuesque build and profile that would make a father welcome him into the fold. A straight-A student all through high school. Graduated with honors from the University of Maryland. This was the ideal package. This kid had it all. So why?

Why the kidnapping? Why the rape? Why the torture and violent murder? It was all so unnecessary. All so meaningless, pointless, senseless. But there had to be a reason for it. Even if that reason was all about him; his sick wishes and desires. His sexual urges that a normal girl could never fulfill, willingly. His need for control; power over another. His desire and need to perform acts of cruelty. He enjoyed it. He was still enjoying it. Yes, this was definitely all about him.

This was a cut and dry case. He had already admitted that he did it. He killed them. There was enough DNA evidence alone to put him away for the rest of his life. He had been caught red-handed trying to sell Cassi's laptop. He had already admitted to the abductions, the rapes, and the murders. He wanted the glory for that, the notoriety. But now, obviously under the guidance of his legal team, he was claiming that voices had made him do it. Typical, he was entering an insanity plea, in the hope of escaping the death sentence. *We'll see about that,* Margo thought to herself.

Dan Larsen, the defense attorney, was a pompous over-dressed peacock. He paraded himself daily in expensive suits with contrasting shirts and loud ties. He wore matching diamond cufflinks and tie pin. His hair was obviously dyed, probably from a box. The color was slightly too dark for a man of his years, and conspicuously devoid of any gray. It was styled in a way as to camouflage an exposed skull cap of pink skin. Margo imagined it lifting up, like a flip-top trashcan lid, in a sudden breeze. There was little, if anything, about this man Margo approved of. His obnoxious mannerisms, his flamboyant attire, his pious, self-absorbed attitude towards others, all served to enrage her. That, and the fact he was defending the man who had brutally murdered her daughter. She watched as he patted Fulton affectionately on the back in a comforting manner, leaning to whisper something in his ear. Almost immediately Fulton's expression changed to one of sadness and remorse. He hung his head. "So, you think you're a director, do you?" Margo said to Larsen, under her breath.

"I beg your pardon?" Jim's voice startled her. Margo turned to see Jim seated on the bench beside her. He was flanked by an overdressed Brigitte, sporting a large-brimmed hat and oversized sunglasses.

"Not you!" she snapped. She gave Brigitte a sideways glance and turned to Jim. "You didn't tell her this was a closed-door hearing? There aren't any cameras in here. Who the hell is she dressed up for?"

"There are still photographers outside," Jim whispered. He rubbed his eyes tiredly. Poor Jim; Margo sometimes forgot that this involved him, too. He reached down and took Margo's hand. "How are you holding up? I've called. You never seem to be home."

"I have a few projects I'm working on. Just trying to stay busy." She smiled up at him. "Thanks for caring."

"I never stopped," he said, a little louder than Margo thought he should. It was a little louder than Brigitte thought he should, too, apparently. Margo could feel her elbow through Jim. "You don't need to be here," Margo heard him say in a low voice. Brigitte mumbled something back, incoherent to Margo. Jim replaced Margo's hand back in her lap and patted it affectionately. He replaced his own hands with his fingers intertwined back in his own lap.

Margo was not sure what to expect from the hearing. She knew the reason they were here, though. Simon Fulton wanted his day in court. He wanted the lights, the cameras, the action. He wanted the world to know what he had done. There was enough evidence to hang, electrocute, and give him a lethal injection, all at the same time. Yet he wanted a trial. He wanted to tell his story to the world, and there was only one way to get his wish. He had to have a defense: insanity. Both sides wielded paperwork filled with medical and psychological facts from 'experts' to enhance their case. Margo sat mesmerized as the lawyers bantered back and forth about evidence from his past that had given clear indications that this was a boy greatly in need of help. How he was not responsible for his actions. How he had suffered greatly when his parents divorced at the age of three. How he had witnessed his mother being beaten by an ex-boyfriend. How he had been abused by a camp leader when he was twelve. How someone should have known there was something wrong when he caught and skinned a neighbor's cat when he was fourteen. How through it all he had been accompanied by the voice of an imaginary accomplice he called Luke. How Luke had been his only friend and companion for many years. Fulton's attorneys tried tirelessly to sell the crazy plea in spite of endless evidence to the contrary submitted by long time family friend, State Prosecutor Jack Ross.

"Your Honor," Ross pleaded, "I have a pile of photographs here obtained from former high school and college buddies and ex-girlfriends. He's laughing and smiling in every one of them. There is no sign of the manic depressive the defense is making him out to be. I have a copy of an audition tape the defendant made when he was twelve for a Nickelodeon TV show. This audition was taped two weeks after he returned from the camp where this alleged sexual abuse took place, at the hands of a camp director whose name no one can remember. As for the Luke character, I ask you, would you be auditioning for *Nick at Night* if your best friend was the Lord of the Undead? What about high school? The defendant played three years of football. What position did Luke play? Was he sitting on the bleachers? Not one kid from the defendant's high school or college can remember ever hearing him mention Luke. What about Joel

Davis, his accomplice in Arizona? This was a college buddy. Joel's mother told us that her son was driving to California to try and get work in Hollywood. He was an aspiring actor. She said that he called her the day after he left and told her that he wasn't alone because one of his friends from school had decided, at the last minute, to come with him. So she didn't have to worry about him. She couldn't remember the name of the boy, but she recognizes the defendant from pictures she received in the mail from Joel. They were friends. Yet he shot him in the head in cold blood when Joel tried to untie Meghan Maddox' hands."

Ross returned to his desk and took a sip from a glass of water. He raised his hand to indicate there was more to come, and took another sip. "Your Honor," he said, putting down the glass, "I have here the transcripts of the defendant's verbal statement. I would like to read it to the court, if I may." The judge nodded her assent.

Jim reached across and took Margo's hand tightly in his own. Margo sensed that he was shielding her from what was to come. She had wanted to know everything that had happened, but no one would tell her anything. Now she was going to find out, and she didn't know if she was ready to hear it.

Ross looked in their direction and then in the direction of the Maddox'. His expression was one of pure sorrow. He really did not want to do this. Margo looked over at her old friend, Jerri. They had not spoken since the murders. Margo could tell from her expression that she did not know what to expect, either.

"We were heading west on I-45 when we saw a couple of girls in a Mustang. They were really good-looking, especially the one in the passenger seat with the dark hair. We tried to keep up with them, but they lost us. We pulled off the road at one of those western steak houses about twenty miles outside Phoenix and saw the Mustang in the parking lot. When we went inside we saw the girls at a table and we asked if we could join them. They said they were just going to eat and leave, so thanks, but no thanks. It kinda pissed me off. I knocked over the blonde girl's drink on purpose. Then I told her I'd go to the bar and get her a new one. I got her a new drink and I put some Roofies in it. I gave it to her and then we left the bar and waited for them in the parking lot. I put quite a bit in so I knew it wouldn't be long. Me and Joel had used that shit quite a few times when we were in college. While we waited, I cut one of their tires. When they came out, the blonde one was staggering and the dark-haired one was trying to help her. We went up and asked them if they needed any help. The dark-haired one said they were fine, that her friend just felt ill. They were gonna be fine. Then she saw that the tire was flat. Her friend started throwing up all over herself. I offered to drop them at their hotel, then they could get a cab back to the car in the morning. She went for it. So we got in the car; Joel was driving and I offered the dark-haired one a drink. I put some Rohypnol in it. Not much, just enough to make it easier, you know. She was really hot. I didn't want her to be out. I wanted her to react a little bit. She wouldn't drink it. Then she noticed that we weren't heading for Phoenix and she started yelling. That's when I pulled out the gun and pointed it at her friend. I told her to shut up or I'd blow her friend's head off. Joel was kind of freakin' out. He didn't even know I had a gun. We drove to a field somewhere. The blonde one was out cold so we just left her in the back seat. We pulled the other one out of the car. I told her we were just going to have a little fun. She was crying, so I asked her, "What's the matter? You like to have fun, don't you?" She started screaming, so I had to hit her a couple of times. I made her take off her clothes. I told her if she did what I told her she'd be okay. Then I raped her, and then I let Joel have her. When we were done, we left her laying on the ground while we grabbed a couple of beers from the car. We waited for the blonde to come round a little, but she didn't. So I had Joel hold the gun to her friend's head, and forced the brunette to give me head. When she finished she spat at me. I beat the crap out of her for that. It felt really good. Then I started getting these really violent thoughts, and I just kind of went with them. When I was finished I had another beer. The dark-haired girl kept crying and begging me to just let them go. She kept promising she wouldn't say anything to anyone; please, please, please, blah, blah, blah. I kept telling her to shut up, but she wouldn't. She kept crying and begging and pleading. It was pissing me off. So I hit her some more. I was sitting on her chest with the gun poked in her cheek. She kept telling me that she'd do whatever I wanted, just don't kill her, please don't kill her. I put the gun in her mouth to shut her up, but she kept shrieking. Then I saw her panties laying there. I had her arms pinned with my knees, so she couldn't move. I started to poke the panties into her mouth. I used the barrel of the gun to pack them into her throat. It was nearly dark out now, but I could see she was turning a weird color. I'd always wanted to see what happened to a person's face when they were choked to death. You know, to see if it was like in the movies. She was biting so hard on the barrel that she was busting her own teeth. Then after a minute or two she stopped fighting. She just kind of went limp. So we had the last two beers and I smoked a couple of cigarettes. Her eyes were open. Even in the dark I could see them staring at me. It got to me. So I put my cigarette out in one of them; I think it was the right. Then I got the idea to make it look like a satanic-type killing. So I carved a pentagram into her forehead."

"You motherfucker! I'm gonna rip you apart!" Jim's screams brought Margo out of her trance. She was suddenly aware of Jim being pinned to the ground beneath three court officers. He had almost made it across the room. He was escorted from the court, with Brigitte following close behind. Simon Fulton was smiling.

"Your Honor," Ross concluded, "the details of this case will be made public if this case goes to trial. The wounds of these families will be reopened and have salt rubbed deep into them. The reputations and memories of the victims will be bandied about by the defense. This is not insanity your honor, just plain evil. The evidence shows guilt. The defendant pleaded guilty. You have no choice but to throw this insanity plea out."

"Mr. Ross, you will do well to remember that this is my courtroom, and I, Mr. Ross, always have a choice."

Margo stared long and hard at Judge Mohen's stony face. This was horrible. She knew Cassi's death must have been brutal, but that? You wouldn't kill a dog like that. This was her baby. She shouldn't have died like that. She shouldn't have died period. Now this monster was going to claim insanity to avoid the death sentence and gain notoriety. The judge was going to become a household name because of this high profile case. The tabloids would splash the girls' lives and deaths all over their front pages. They would print vivid details of the physical, sexual, and mental torture they had endured. Their entire lives would only be remembered as the grisly details of their deaths. Margo tasted vomit in the back of her throat. That could not happen. There could not be a trial. There *would not* be a trial.

Chapter Twenty-Eight

Jason Lawless bit into his bagel and cream cheese. He chewed slowly as he watched the tape of last night's edition of *Lawless in LA*. The police chief was trying to defend the officers involved in the latest beating of an African American youth in custody for possession of crack cocaine.

"Good show last night, hon," his wife, Jill, said proudly. "Especially the story on the cab drivers being set up for mugging."

"I don't know. It seemed a bit same old-same old." He took a sip of his coffee and another bite of his bagel. "The ratings are down by eighteen percent this month. We need some news."

"Well, it had everything in it. Sex, drugs, murder, police brutality!" Jill offered.

"Like I said, same old-same old." Jason rubbed his eyes. "Sometimes I think we should get out of L.A. Think of the kid," he said, eyeing a large bump in Jill's abdomen.

"We grew up in L.A., and we turned out okay," Jill crooned.

"There weren't any snipers in kindergarten when we grew up." He patted her bump affectionately. "What do you think, Jason Junior? Want to move to Aspen?"

"Yeah, like you could handle snow for more than a week at a time," Jill said, smacking him over the head with an assortment of envelopes. "And I told you already, this is Jill junior."

"You got the mail? Anything for me in there?" He held out his hand.

Jill scanned the fronts of the envelopes one at a time. "Bill!" she said, placing the letter to the back. "Bill! Bill! Bill! Check for me!" She smiled at Jason. "Ooh, here's a hand-written one for you." She placed a letter-sized manila envelope in his hand. "Who's it from?"

"Don't know." Jason turned the envelope over and back again. "There's no return address." He used his cream cheese knife to open it. Inside were two eight-by-eleven sheets of paper, on one of which were the scanned images of two drivers' licenses. Pasted to the other sheet were paragraphs clipped from a local newspaper. One was the news story of two men found dead in a warehouse; the other the story of a man who appeared to have jumped from a parking lot roof. Beneath the clippings were printed the words: *"We are sweeping the trash from the streets of L.A. If you don't air this story, we'll send it to someone else who will."* Jason looked in the envelope for a clue of who might have sent this. There, stuck in the corner was a black and silver business card. He held it up for Jill to see.

"Oh, my God, Jason! Call the police." Jill picked up the phone and handed it to her husband.

"Hang on a minute." He held up his hand, pondering the situation. "You read it. If I don't use this, they'll just give it to someone else."

"You can't put this on the air! These people are murderers!" Jill pushed the phone in his direction. "Jason, you have to call the police."

"Wait a minute — wait a minute!" His mind was racing. "What if I air it and then hand it over to the police."

"Jason! This is an ongoing police investigation. You're withholding possible evidence!" Once again she offered him the phone.

"You're right, you're right!" he said, accepting the phone. Shit! Why did he have to marry a goddamn lawyer!

"Make the call, Jason!" Jill said, walking out of the room. "I'll call you from the office." She blew him a kiss. "Do the right thing." She slipped out the door. He waited for the click of the latch. Jason dialed; a man answered.

"Larry Birch."

"Larry, it's me, Jason. Listen. Forget the section we were going to run about the hookers tonight. I've got the story of the year. This is big, Larry!"

Chapter Twenty-Nine

"Where's the good bottle opener?' Rick Sawyer asked, looking at the broken cork.

"That is the good bottle opener," his wife called from the kitchen. "Did you bust the cork again?"

"No," he lied. He managed to re-screw the remaining piece of cork and pull it from the bottle.

Angela emerged from the kitchen holding a large bowl of paella. She placed it carefully in the center of the table. "Where are the napkins?" she asked. Rick shrugged. "Jesus, Rick! I only asked you to set the table and open the wine." She walked back into the kitchen muttering to herself in Spanish.

"Hey!" Rick called out. "I know what you just said."

"And yet," Angela said, as she re-emerged from the kitchen smiling, "the cork is still in your hand."

Rick put his arms around his petite wife and pulled her close. He kissed her neck. "I love it when you talk dirty to me in Spanish."

"Yeah, well maybe those Hawaiian boys will like it, too," she teased.

"I'm not worried," Rick said mockingly. "Two girls normally get hit on by two guys. Since the girl you're going with is three hundred pounds, and nobody wants to get stuck with the fat chick … I think you're safe."

"Are you sure about that?" she teased. "You know Hawaiian men like a little meat on their women."

"Well in that case, skinny, maybe you're ruining her chances. Either way, I feel secure." He kissed her softly on the lips. "Where's the remote?"

Rick walked to the coffee table while Angela began ladling the rice concoction onto the plates. "I suppose you want to watch that dumb-ass show," he said, returning to the table.

"It's only dumb-ass because it holds the LAPD accountable," Angela retorted. "I don't get upset when it talks about the school district."

"Yeah," Rick said sarcastically. "I've noticed."

He began pushing a series of buttons on the remote. The television screen suddenly flashed to a blue screen and then various images began to appear, rapidly.

"What are you doing?" Angela asked. "Stop flicking through the channels like that! It's on thirteen."

"I know," he lied again. He entered the channel's numbers, and the opening credits for *Lawless in LA* appeared on the screen.

Something about Jason Lawless' smug expression got on Rick's nerves. He appeared to look even oilier tonight, Rick thought, as the image of Jason Lawless sitting behind a desk came into view. There was something familiar, and yet different, about the set tonight. Same old desk. Same asinine presenter. Different backdrop. The usual backdrop was a white screen with a pair of broken police handcuffs on it, denoting the lawless situation in L.A. Tonight, however, the backdrop was black, with what appeared to be a pair of silver justice scales and a banner beneath it. The word 'exclusive' was stamped diagonally across it in bold print.

"Shit," Rick said almost inaudibly.

"What's the matter?" Angela asked concerned. She looked at the screen as the images of two driver's licenses flashed on-screen. Rick recognized them immediately.

"Shit!" Rick repeated.

"It appears as though there is a new sheriff in town," Lawless' voice droned in the background. Suddenly the image changed to one of a hand-written note. "We were contacted here at the station this morning by a group going by the name of 'The Cleaning Crew'."

"Shit."

Chapter Thirty

"I told you, it came in the mail this morning, addressed to me." Lawless casually took a draw from his cigarette. "You can see, it says right on it, if I don't show it they'll just give it to someone else." He flicked the ash on the studio floor.

"This is an ongoing investigation," Sanchez said, in his best bad-cop voice. "You could be charged with obstruction of justice or interfering with police matters."

"Who's interfering?" Lawless sounded totally unconcerned. "I gave you guys everything I have. I'm not hiding anything."

"You should have called us before you aired this," Sanchez continued. "Like I said, this is an ongoing investigation."

"Like I said, it was addressed to me. I have the right to show it if I want. What happened to free speech? You can't censor me." He dropped his cigarette butt and put it out with his foot defiantly.

"No, but maybe the D.A. can," Sanchez countered.

"Well, he can take it up with the studio lawyers." He nodded to his right. "Here they come right now."

Three extremely well-dressed men in designer suits marched boldly toward them. Rick groaned. "Come on, Lawless, we're talking murder here."

"Hey, I didn't murder anyone," Lawless grinned. "And if there's someone out there taking care of the scum of society, then that's news guys. That's what I do. I report the news."

"We're just asking to be in the loop, Lawless," Rick protested. "Just show us what you've got before you air it."

"What? So you can confiscate it?" Lawless laughed. "You can take it up with these guys. I think we're done here, fellas." Lawless rose and turned to face the lawyers.

"Gentlemen!" The first of the three approaching men sang out. "As an executive of this studio, and therefore a client of the law firm of Wallace, Cohen, and Gonzalez, Mr. Lawless won't be able to say anything else without an attorney present."

Lawless shrugged. "This case has even got my wife pissed at me."

"You and me both," Rick grumbled.

Chapter Thirty-One

"How many are there?" Peta asked.

"Thirty-six total," Raul checked his watch. "They should be pulling out soon." He had become accustomed to their schedule now. They had been watching them for three weeks. Chavez and Dix rode out here to the Roadhouse twice a week and met up with this crew. Although they always separated after the meeting, he knew they were all a part of the same gang. He suspected Chavez and Dix were probably collecting money or making a payment for drugs on the first day, and either picking up or delivering the drugs on the second.

Luis Delgado, his third person of interest, rode with the gang now, for whatever reason, but at one time the three of them had been inseparable. They had been former members together of an earlier gang known as the Sirocco, out of the Bay Area. Raul's sister, much to his despair, had been dating one of its members, Joey Nunos.

Estella was a pretty, intelligent, outgoing young woman. She was working full time as a computer repair consultant, while putting herself through college for technical art. Raul remembered the first time she brought Joey home. He was concerned about the obvious gang-related tattoos that covered the young man's body. Estella didn't seem to care. She was smitten with him. Within a month she had moved out of the home she shared with Raul and their mother and into a small apartment with Joey.

The last time Raul saw his sister alive he noticed how much her interaction with Joey had changed her. She was wearing lots of makeup, and not at all flattering. Her eyes and lips were outlined with a heavy black liner. She proudly showed off her new 'tramp stamp,' in the small of her back, clearly visible above the low-cut, tight jeans and the elaborately-styled Sirocco on the back of her neck. When Raul had expressed his displeasure at her appearance, she reminded him of the fact that she was twenty-years-old and didn't need his approval. She had stormed out of the house without telling him or their mother goodbye.

Soon after, Joey was imprisoned for peddling heroine. Over the phone, Raul had tried to persuade Estella to move back home, but he suspected her pride was the reason she refused. A few days after the conversation with his little sister, the police called to say that her car had been found abandoned in a supermarket parking lot in East L.A., and she hadn't reported for work or college in two days. Three days later the police called again, this time to say they had found Estella. They had used dental records to identify her. From what they could tell of the remains, after being raped multiple times, she had apparently been bound at the wrists and dragged behind a vehicle through the high desert just south of Sacramento. There were no other injuries to the body, such as puncture wounds or gunshots, and so they concluded that this was the cause of death.

Raul had gone insane upon hearing this news. He knew none of this would ever have happened if she had not been involved with Joey. Computer techs and art students did not get gang-banged and then dragged through the desert to their deaths. He knew that this was probably someone getting back at Joey through his girl. Raul used his connections in the prison to find out where Joey was being held. He had every intention of paying him a visit, only to discover that Joey had conveniently hung himself the day after Estella's body was found.

Forensics showed, however, that he had help in his own demise. Apparently, when Joey had been picked up he had, for whatever reason, given the police the name of one of his accomplices, Danny Chavez, resulting in his arrest. So it was obvious: Joey had to die. Estella's death just added insult to injury. Her death was the prelude to Joey's inevitable, fatal punishment. They wanted to let him know they were coming.

Peta and Raul watched silently as Dix and Chavez swigged beer from bottles and took hits from a joint. They laughed loudly, profanities streaming from their mouths. The gang emerged from inside the bar. Most of them walked off in the direction of their bikes, while a few hovered around the front of the building. Dix and Chavez were joined by a third man. Peta noticed Raul's jaw tighten as Delgado joined in with the conversation.

"They'll be splitting up soon," she observed. Raul was silent, deep in thought. "I think I have enough pictures now. Are you ready to head back?" His silence bothered her.

The gang began firing up their motorcycles. A couple of men still standing in front of the building waved to Dix and Chavez as they walked away. Dix, Chavez, and Delgado waved back. Delgado carried on his conversation. He lit up a cigarette. Raul leaned forward in his seat, his eyes burning. "He's not going with them!" he stated.

"What?" Peta asked a little surprised by his sudden eagerness.

"He's not leaving! The three of them are staying together!" Raul leaned over and opened his glove box. Peta saw the 357 Magnum inside. Raul slapped the door shut as though he had just been checking to see that the gun was in there.

"Raul, what are you doing? We're just here to track their movements, remember?" Peta could feel her stomach tightening.

"Peta, you need to get out now," he said coolly.

"What? I'm not getting out! What are you thinking about?" She was desperately trying to find the voice of reason. "Raul, we can't make a move without the rest of the group."

The motorcycle gang started to pull out of the parking lot. The pack was quite impressive and very intimidating as they pulled out onto the highway. Raul looked back at the three men on the porch. Delgado threw his cigarette butt to the floor and crushed it with his heel. They started to walk in the direction of the parking lot.

"Peta, get out!" Raul yelled.

"Why? What the hell are you going to do?" Peta started to feel frantically in her purse for her phone. She had to call Doug. He would talk some sense into him.

"Peta!" Raul yelled. "This might be my only chance to get all three of them alone! Get out!"

"No! Peta spat back. "I'm coming with you!"

"Get out!" Raul sounded a little deranged.

"No!" Peta was determined to win on this one. Raul must have seen that in her eyes.

"Fine; fucking stay!" he snapped.

He watched as the three men started up their bikes and pulled out of the parking lot in the opposite direction the gang had gone. He put the truck into drive and started out after them slowly. Once on the highway he put his foot down on the gas. Now he was hunting. There was very little traffic on the road at this time in the morning; there was very little traffic on this road period. He looked in the rear view — nothing. Straight ahead he could see the bikes. He accelerated slightly. He was gaining on them nicely. They couldn't have been doing more than sixty.

"Put your belt on," he said calmly to Peta.

"What are you going to do?" Peta looked anxiously across at him.

"I'm going bowling," he said through a sick smile. He put his foot down on the gas hard.

Peta watched as the needle rose on the speedometer: Seventy-five, eighty, eighty-five. They were on top of them now. Peta could read the license plate of the last bike. She could see the emblem on the back of his leather vest, the silhouette of a large cat, and the word 'Panthers' on the bottom. The name Danny was on the back of his helmet. So this was Chavez. His long hair was in a braid flying back in the air. They were real close. Chavez turned his head to see who was coming up behind him so quickly. He waved for Raul to go past him. Raul pulled to the left of him, and for a moment Peta actually thought that he was in fact going to overtake him. Until he suddenly yanked the wheel to the right violently. The truck struck the middle of the bike hard. Peta thought it actually went up into the air before crashing into the desert tumbling in slow motion. Chavez seemed to become a part of the mangled machine, tumbling with it. The second rider saw what had happened in his rear view, and assuming it was an accident, had begun to slow down. Raul hit him in the rear so hard, the whole bike went up and over the top of the truck, smashing Peta's side of the windshield. She screamed in horror. Raul's eyes were locked icily on the last bike. He was doing over ninety miles an hour now. The last rider realized too late that he was, in fact, a target. By the time he tried to accelerate, Raul was already on him, striking him hard on the side, sending him crashing into the desert like Chavez. Raul stepped hard on the brake and stopped a hundred yards up the road. He turned the wheel frantically, making a fast U-turn. He came up on the first bike almost immediately. The rider was either unconscious or dead. Raul didn't much care which. He jumped out of the truck and ran through the desert to him. Once there he pulled a pair of cuffs from his back pocket, and fastened the man's hands behind his back. Leaving him there in the desert, he ran back to the truck. He would come back and get him after he had secured the other two, he decided. He drove the short distance back to the second bike. The rider looked like he was in a bad way. There was a lot of blood. Seeing as he was on the side of the road anyway, after Raul had cuffed him, he picked him up and threw him over his shoulder. He managed to carry him the short distance to the truck, where Peta was now standing.

"Open the tailgate," he instructed her. Peta obeyed without question. He threw the man he now recognized to be Dix into the back of the truck, who landed with a thud and a loud groan. "Get back in the truck," he ordered Peta.

When Raul got to the last bike, he was surprised to find Chavez conscious. He was groaning loudly. His left leg was broken in a couple of pieces; a large piece of bone was jutting out of his shin through his denim jeans.

"You crazy bastard!" he yelled at Raul. "Look at my leg! Look what you did to my leg! Who are you? What the fuck do you want, man?"

"I want to make sure you die in fucking agony, you piece of shit!" Raul spat at him. "I've waited a long time for this."

"Fuck you!" Chavez screamed. "You can kill me, but you're gonna get yours, asshole." Chavez seemed to be almost chuckling.

"Not before I ..." Raul paused. *What the hell?* The sound of motorcycle engines was getting louder. It was coming from the direction the pack had been headed. Raul heard a guttural laugh coming from Chavez. He was holding something up in the air.

"It's a fucking pager, man! It tells my boys that something's going down and I need backup." He chuckled again. "You're fucked now!" The bikes were getting closer. Raul could see them. They would be here in less than a minute. He ran the short distance to the truck.

"Get down!" he screamed at Peta. She lay across the seat obediently. He hit the button on the glove box. Nothing happened. The motorcycle engines were really loud now. He hit the button again, nothing. The engines, now all around the truck, were deafening. Frantically, he punched the button again hard and it swung open. He grabbed the Magnum and cocked the hammer.

From outside the truck he heard the distinctive sound of someone racking a shotgun.

"Drop the gun, motherfucker!"

Chapter Thirty-Two

As soon as he dropped the gun, Raul felt a tremendous pain at the base of his skull. Everything went black.

"Throw him in the back with Roadrash!" the guy with the gold earrings hollered. "Put Danny in there, too. Lou, you okay to ride my bike?"

Delgado held up his handcuffed hands. Immediately, two men were on the scene, one with a large chisel, the other wielding a heavy mallet. Delgado pulled his hands as far apart as he could, placing the chain across a large rock. The first man placed the chisel on the links and the second man brought down the mallet with a loud blow, breaking apart the chain. Delgado held up his free hands triumphantly.

"I am now!" he replied. He was covered in blood, but didn't appear to have sustained any physical damage other than a nasty gash to the forehead. He nodded and walked in the direction of the already running motorcycle nearby. The man with the gold earrings walked to the passenger side of the truck. He pointed the pump-action shotgun directly at Peta's face.

"Get behind the wheel," he ordered. Peta slid across the bench seat into place behind the wheel. "Drive!" he yelled, jumping into the cab with ease. He held the shotgun in a way that told Peta to just do as she was told. "Follow the bikes. If you do one thing wrong, they'll be wiping the inside of your face off the dash."

Peta followed the bikes through the desert area of southern California. They rode with purpose, as though they were on a mission, never dropping below sixty miles per hour. The man with the earrings was silent the whole time. Peta snatched a glimpse of him whenever she could. His face looked slightly familiar. Like an actor she couldn't quite place, in a role she couldn't quite recall. His face was good-looking, but hard and serious. He might have looked less dangerous without the wild long black hair and thick beard. They gave him a kind of Charles Manson quality, which Peta found unnerving. This was a man who had seen a lot of violence, she guessed, some of which he wore in his eyes. She did not doubt for one minute that this man was capable of blowing her head off. In fact, she was quite confident that, at the end of this journey, he had every intention of doing just that. It was funny; a year ago she would have been crying like a baby right now. She was different then, vulnerable, weak. Chico had been her strength. Now she was in charge, responsible for her life, for her death. She had had the chance to get out of the truck, walk away, avoid all this. She had made the decision to stay. She had chosen this, and she was not scared. Death did not scare her, life did. Anyone can die.

The bikes came to a halt inside a small canyon. Peta looked around. There was absolutely nothing to see, just the walls of the canyon. This was as good a place to die as any, she told herself.

"Pull up behind them," the guy with the gold earrings snapped, nodding toward a small group of bikes to their right. She followed his directions, and then turned off the engine. She purposely left the keys dangling in the ignition. Maybe she and Raul would get a chance to make a break for the truck, she told herself without much hope. "Get out!" he said venomously. Peta did as she was told.

A group of the bikers had collected around the truck. A few of them were helping Chavez and Dix down from the back. Dix was conscious now, and apparently able to stand up unassisted. Up close Peta could see why his nickname was Roadrash. His face was either badly pock-marked, or else this guy had been in a fire; it was hard to tell which. His clothes were torn and covered in blood, but it was not evident where he was injured. *These are some tough guys,* she thought to herself.

"Get him out of there!" the guy with the gold earrings shouted.

Another biker jumped up into the back of the truck. He rolled Raul's still unconscious body toward the end and then pushed him off hard, so he landed with a thud on the stony ground. He didn't move, and Peta could see blood at the back of his head where one of the bikers had hit him earlier with the butt of a shotgun.

"Raul!" she screamed, and tried to move forward, but the guy with the earrings grabbed her by the hair and yanked her back.

"Did I tell you to fucking move?" he snarled. He released his grip on Peta and strode over to where Raul lay. Cautiously moving his hands over Raul's body, he pulled a set of keys from his front pocket, and threw them to a younger man with a noticeable lack of tattoos. He shouted, "Get those bracelets off them!" The younger man ran first to Delgado and relieved him of his matching bangles. Then he ran over to Dix, who was standing close by, and who had already managed to free one hand from the cuffs. He held up the wrist that bore the still-fastened manacles eagerly.

The guy with the earrings turned his attention back to Raul. "Wake him up!" he yelled.

"I'll do it!" Delgado shouted. He moved forward and unzipped his fly. To Peta's horror, he began to urinate in Raul's face. The gang members howled. Raul didn't move. Delgado lifted Raul's head up by the hair and slapped him hard across the face. When that got no response, he repeated the action. Raul's eyes opened a little. Then Delgado kicked him hard in the back. "Wake up, motherfucker!" he shouted through clenched teeth. Raul groaned in agony. He was awake.

"Okay, back off!" the guy with the earrings said.

"Are you fucking kidding me? I'm gonna kill this guy!" Delgado challenged.

"I said back off!" Peta could tell by the way he didn't have to raise his voice that this was the boss. "He can't talk dead, asshole!" He stood over Raul. "Who are you? Who sent you?"

"Nobody," Raul answered with a groan.

The guy with the gold earrings raised his right fist and brought it down hard on Raul's jaw. "Try again," he said. "Who are you?"

"Nobody," Raul repeated.

Once again he struck Raul in the face, this time harder. "We can do this nice, or we can do this nasty," the guy with the earrings told him. "Now who are you?"

"I told you, nobody!" Raul answered.

"Drag him over there," the guy with the earrings ordered.

Two men grabbed Raul by the arms and dragged him through the dirt to the trunk of a dead mesquite tree. This was something they had done before, because without any further direction they draped him across the trunk in a way that the back of his knees were on the tree and his heels were in the dirt. Two other bikers ran forward and held his feet firmly against the ground.

The guy with the earrings walked over slowly. Once again he leaned over Raul. "Last chance. Who are you?"

"I forgot," Raul said defiantly. "I must've banged my head."

"Really. Maybe this will jolt your memory." The guy with the earrings raised his right foot.

Peta screamed loudly as he brought the heel of his boot down hard on Raul's left leg. The breaking of bone could be heard over her cries of anguish. Raul let out an animalistic howl of pain, like a bear in a trap.

"No! No!" Peta cried, running forward and throwing herself on top of Raul.

"Get her the fuck out of here!" the guy with the earrings hollered. He reached down and grabbed hold of Peta's jacket, pulling her up violently. "If you don't shut your fucking ..." He paused. "Where the fuck did you get this?" he demanded through clenched teeth.

"What?" Peta sobbed.

"This!" he said, turning the lapel of her jacket over roughly to expose a small gold pin. "Where did you fucking get it?"

"I ... I ... We're ... I'm in a group," she said meekly.

"Who gave you the pin?" he demanded.

"Someone in the group." Peta stared up at him with instant recognition.

"Oh, my God! You're Lena's boy! David Solomon!" she whispered.

"Who are you? Why are you here?" he asked Peta.

"They raped and killed his sister," Peta said matter-of-factly.

"Who did? When was this?" Solomon looked baffled. "My guys don't hurt women," he said, releasing his hold on her.

"Two years ago," Raul said through panting breath. He was in a lot of pain. "They were in Sirocco then."

"I was in Sirocco." A big man with a shaved head stepped forward. "I don't remember anybody being raped. We didn't do that shit."

"There were four of them working together, running drugs," Raul continued. "One of them was Joey Nunos. My sister was living with him."

"Come on, Dave! Are you going to listen to this fucking jerk?" Delgado shouted suddenly to Solomon. "Fuck the Siroccos, man; this is the Panthers. This motherfucker tried to kill us." Delgado reached around the back of his jeans and pulled out a handgun. At the same time the big man with the shaved head racked his shotgun.

"Drop it, Delgado!" he said. "I want to know what happened. I knew Joey real well. I taught him to ride a bike. He was like a kid brother to me."

Delgado dropped the gun and Solomon picked it up. "Go on," he nodded to Raul.

"When Nunos got arrested, he dropped Chavez' name, who got picked up, too," Raul continued. "Dix and Delgado were pissed 'cause it cost them a lot of money. Chavez was being held in the same facility as Joey. They managed to get money to him to pay people to whack Joey and make it look like he hung himself. But before they took care of him, they grabbed my sister from a supermarket parking lot and took her out in the desert. They raped her and tied her wrists together and dragged her through the desert behind their truck." He paused to get a breath. The pain from his leg was excruciating. "Before Joey was killed, they showed him a picture of Estella after they had finished with her. They put it in his shirt pocket when he was dead."

"Hey! I didn't fucking kill nobody!" Chavez' voice whined. "It was those two who did the girl!"

"Shut the fuck up, Danny!" Dix shouted.

"No way, man! I'm not taking shit for you two!" Chavez was sitting on the ground propped up against a rear truck tire. Someone had tried to make a splint for his leg, but with the piece of bone still sticking out it was pretty pointless. He winced as he tried to pull himself up higher. "They told me to take care of Joey and I did. It was fucking Louie calling the shots! I just did what they said! Joey was a piece of shit anyway! He was too busy playing fucking house with his bitch to notice he was being followed around by the pigs, man. He could've got us all hung. He had it fucking coming! I don't give a ..."

The sound of the shotgun report made Peta jump and cup her ears. The huge hole that suddenly appeared in Chavez' chest made her gasp. The back end of the truck listed to one side.

"I'm sorry about that," the bald-headed man said. "I hope you've got a spare."

"What the fuck?! What the fuck?!" Dix suddenly became quite agitated. "You fucking killed him, man! He was one of us!"

"No," The bald-headed man replied. "He was one of you. Don't put yourself in the same class as me, asshole. I spent the last two years of my life thinking that I was responsible for Joey hanging himself. That if I didn't introduce him to the gang, he might still be alive. If I'd known what happened, all three of you would have been dead two years ago." He turned to face Solomon. "Hey, Boss, I did what I had to do. You do what you gotta do." He handed him the shotgun.

"Well, first," Solomon said, "Santo and Roadrash are gonna change that tire.

Chapter Thirty-Three

"Thank you, man, I owe you," Raul said.

"Consider it payback. You took care of business for me in L.A. That was big, man. You saved my sister, and got rid of the pieces of shit that took my brother out. I owe you for that." He looked down at the small gold pin on his vest. "Tell my mother she did a good thing sending me this. It saved your life."

"I just wish we had a card," Peta sighed.

"We do," Solomon said, fishing in his back pocket. He pulled out a tattered wallet, and flipped it open. Peta could see family pictures inside. From one of the slots he pulled an instantly recognizable black card. "Mom sent me a couple of these with the pin. I think she made me an honorary member." He shrugged.

"You can't use that!" Peta said, concerned. "Your prints are on it."

"Nah! You just wipe the surface with a rag dipped in gasoline and it smears the prints. Dissolves the oil in 'em," he said, winking. He turned to Peta. "Enjoy the rest of the show, and then get this guy to a hospital. We'll get rid of any tracks after you leave, and I'll make sure the card is somewhere it will be found. Adios." He shook both their hands and turned to leave.

They both watched as he mounted his bike and sped away, back down the dirt track toward the canyon, a small cloud of dust the only indication of his whereabouts. Peta turned to see Raul's face in contortions.

"What's the matter? Are you in pain?" she asked concerned.

"Yeah, but that's not it," he answered. "Something smells like piss around here!"

"I'll tell you about that later. Are you ready to leave?" Peta asked gently.

"Yeah," Raul replied. "I've seen all I need to see here."

"Okay, I'll take it easy. Hold on." She walked to the front of the truck and climbed into the cab.

Raul winced as the truck lurched forward. Sitting in the back was definitely not a comfortable ride, but he needed to keep his leg straight. He took one last look into the canyon below. It was really quite beautiful to watch the two motorcycles riding in unison, performing perfect figure eights. They moved almost as if in a ballet or an aerial display. Accentuated beautifully by the clouds of dust behind them, thrown up by the bodies of Delgado and Dix.

Chapter Thirty-Four

"Stop telling me to calm down!" Doug said through clenched teeth. "He could have gotten them both killed."

"But he didn't, did he?" Margo countered. "Maybe that's exactly how it was supposed to happen."

"Stop with the 'everything happens for a fucking reason,' bullshit!" Doug said waving her off. "The fact is, he didn't stick to the plan, and he risked Peta's life, as well as his own."

"Hey!" Peta interjected. "I'm a big girl! I could have gotten out of the truck. Nobody held me hostage."

"So why didn't you?" Doug snapped.

"Because then Solomon wouldn't have grabbed her by the neck and seen the pin, and he would have killed Raul," Margo added. "She was supposed to be there," she said smugly.

"You people are out of your fucking minds!" Doug hissed.

"Yeah, but you're the only one acting crazy right now," Georgia said in her mild-mannered, told-you-so kind of way. "Need I remind you we're in a hospital? These damn walls are paper thin. You need to hush up!" She slapped Doug hard on the arm. "That's better," she added. "What time does that fool's show come on?" she asked, picking up the remote from the bed.

"Seven," Raul said sullenly.

"You think he'll put it on the show tonight?" Georgia asked.

"He should. Solomon said he was going to let the police know exactly where to find them before any animals could get at them. Margo met us here last night, and took the IDs. Did you send them right away, Margo?"

"Well, I wiped everything down with alcohol wipes first. Then I put them in with a business card and a short typed note, and took them over to that Fedex office. You know the one I mean, next to the Polish market?" Raul nodded that he did. "Anyway, I didn't put his last name on it, just his first, and the address. I didn't want to draw attention to myself. The guy there told me they could deliver it within the hour."

"How did you not draw attention to yourself?" Doug asked sarcastically. "I mean, is there anyone in the valley who doesn't know who you are?"

"For your information, Doug, I've been driving around this area for the last twenty-five years. Britney and Paris may have a hard time staying incognito, but if you don't want to stand out, you don't. People only know it's me when I want them to know it's me. If you must know," she added, folding her arms, "I had on a blonde wig and sunglasses, t-shirt and jeans, and I paid cash." Doug muttered something to himself that was barely audible.

Right then, the door to the private room opened. Moses stuck his head around the door smiling broadly. "Hey! You got room in here for two more?" He swung the door wide open with his foot to reveal both hands carrying heavy plastic bags full of Chinese food. Bernadette padded in behind him, her arms full of boxes filled with various pastries, and Starbucks coffee in a to-go box. "Bernie figured you could all use something to eat," Moses beamed.

'I know how bad this hospital food is," she said, kissing Raul on the cheek. "Glad to see you're okay, honey."

"Sshh!" Georgia quieted them. "It's on now." Everyone looked for somewhere to sit in the cramped room.

Moses took a seat on the bed clumsily, causing Raul to wince and gasp loudly. "Hey, sorry, man," Moses said with an apologetic smile. Raul nodded his forgiveness.

The titles and credits vanished from the screen to reveal Jason Lawless standing somewhere in the California desert in the black of night. Behind him were numerous police vehicles, lights flashing, and yellow police tape seemed to be draped everywhere, held in place by poles driven into the ground. Huge spotlights stood on tripods, eerily out of place among the cacti and Joshua trees.

"I'm here," Lawless began, "in a barren, desolate area of Death Valley, about three hundred miles east of Fresno, after receiving an anonymous tip. Police arrived here just minutes before my crew in fact, to discover a grisly murder scene, where the bodies of three men were left earlier today. I have here with me Detective Rick Sawyer of the LAPD. Detective Sawyer, can you tell us if this is the work of 'The Cleaning Crew'?"

"The who?" Sawyer asked innocently.

"Is this the same team of vigilantes who took credit on my show for the murders of Cicci, Venetto, and Lewis just two weeks ago?" Lawless pushed the mike into Sawyer's face.

"A full report will be issued as soon as our forensics team has had a chance to go over the evidence. Until that time ..."

"Did they leave a calling card?" Lawless persisted.

"I'm not at liberty to discuss ..."

"How did you know where to look for the bodies?" Lawless continued.

"How did *you* know?" Sawyer countered.

Suddenly the scene was back in the studio, with Lawless seated behind his familiar desk. "That footage was taken in the early morning hours. We received an anonymous tip that led us to the very spot where these three men lost their lives less than twenty-four hours earlier." The faces of the three dead men, apparently clipped from their drivers' licenses, flashed onscreen. The picture then changed to one of the familiar business card. "It appears this is in fact the work of 'The Cleaning Crew,' a vigilante group based right here in L.A. Out of respect for the families and in cooperation with the police we have chosen not to disclose the identities of the victims at this time."

"Where the hell does he get off calling us the damn cleaning crew?" Georgia complained. "Makes us sound like a bunch of damn maids running around!"

"Hey what d'ya expect? The guy's an insensitive prick!" Doug said through a mouth full of noodles. "Hey! Did you get wontons?"

Chapter Thirty-Five

Lester Nichols wiped the dust from the bottles lovingly. This was more than a liquor store to him. This place was a history, geography, and culinary lesson, ready to be taught to anyone willing to learn. Lester knew exactly which area and region every wine in the place came from, especially the French ones. He knew the history of every vineyard in California. He had personally been to most of them. He could tell you which wine went perfectly with which food. He knew which were the good years for a particular label, and the years to avoid. He knew which brandy was the smoothest on the throat, which malt whiskey really could be described as 'fine,' and which rye whiskey never to buy for a friend. He knew it all. The trouble was, nobody really cared. Most people chose their wines by price. They either wanted something cheap to throw on the table when family came over, something in the middle price range to take to a dinner party, or the most expensive to impress their socialite friends or an employer. But they didn't truly care, not the way he did. Not anymore.

This neighborhood had been very different twenty-six years ago when they first bought the store. It had been the home to a thriving business area, with some of the best restaurants in town. Anne had hosted wine tasting parties three times a week back then. They were attended by the city's doctors, lawyers, politicians, and Hollywood's elite. At one time they had even had a small art gallery in the back, where local artists had displayed their work. This place had seen the rise of many nobodies to somebodies over the years. But times change.

As is always the case, newer 'in places' sprout up. The popularity of one place decreases as it increases for another. Although business had remained steady for Lester and Anne, they were no longer in the limelight. The clientele had changed. Lester had made the decision to no longer just sell fine wines, but to introduce some of the cheaper and less popular German and

Australian wines into the inventory. When business started to decline further, he began selling liquor, and sadly, much to his wife's chagrin, beer. She had been visibly distraught the day they had installed the huge refrigerators, which now lined the wall on the left side of the store. When Lester had suggested they sell tobacco, too, she had cried. She wasn't in this for the money, she had told him. Wine was their passion, she had reminded him. Who the hell ever got passionate about Budweiser and Marlboro lights? Lester and the economy had won out, though, and the large cigarette and tobacco case, which hung on the wall behind the cash register, had been a constant reminder to Anne.

Crime in the area had increased, too. Although they were not exactly in a war zone, the existence of local gangs was evident. Graffiti had begun to appear on a regular basis, and many of the business owners, tired of repeatedly repainting, had resigned themselves to the fact that a clean building was merely a blank canvas as far as the taggers were concerned. After their second break-in, Lester had a protective metal screen installed over the front window that he pulled down when the store was closed for the night. He also had extra cameras installed inside and outside the store. Yet another reminder to Anne that their passion was dying.

When the drug dealers arrived it was the last straw for Anne. At her insistence, Lester began looking around for alternate locations for their business. Sadly, the real estate values in their area had plummeted, while it had soared in other, more desirable, areas. The couple had to accept that they were here to stay. Anne decided to become more involved in the community. She hosted drug awareness and crime prevention talks in what was once an art gallery in the back. She became well known to other business owners and law enforcement in the area. In fact, there was always fresh coffee and pastries made available for the officers in the neighborhood. Anne liked to have the police presence, and they appreciated the pastries.

It was after one of their regular coffee and pastry stops that two local officers got into a confrontation with drug dealers, right outside the liquor store. The situation escalated rapidly, and suddenly the police officers found themselves being fired upon. Anne dialed the phone frantically to get help, while Lester watched the ensuing gunfight through the window. When the fracas ended, they ran outside to find two dead drug dealers, one cop dead and the other shot in the leg. Anne had done her best to administer first aid until the ambulance arrived, but there was little she could do for his shattered knee. She could only try to stop the blood flow and give what little comfort she could to the injured officer. Cradling his head in her lap, she had told him how important his and his partner's work had been, and how in debt to them they were. She knew that he needed to hear that. Out of respect, Lester had placed a blanket over the body of the dead police officer to stop the gawking stares from onlookers. The memory haunted Anne. Lester noticed how often she would gaze through the window, sighing heavily, with moist eyes.

Lester wiped the last bottle and replaced it on the shelf. He looked at his watch. "Time," he said softly, walking toward the front door. He flipped the sign over from "Closed" to "Open," and slid the huge bolts back from the top and bottom of the door. He took his place behind the register. The other business owners had laughed at Anne and Lester. They told them that nobody closed for lunch anymore, and they were losing revenue because of it. Anne did not care. They were the only liquor store in the area, and she was closing for lunch. They would have to either come in before twelve for their Marlboros, or come in after one, but she was having lunch with her husband. About a year ago, Anne had opened the door to a waiting customer. When he suddenly pushed the barrel of a gun into her face, she began screaming loudly. Either through panic, or perhaps just to shut her up, the intruder had fired. Lester ran in from the back and found Anne on the floor bleeding from a gunshot to the head. She died before she even made it to the hospital. The surveillance cameras had not caught the man's face and Anne's killer had been walking the streets free for the last six months.

Out of respect for his wife's wishes he had kept the store hours the same. Every day he locked the front door at twelve and went in the back to eat a sandwich he had picked up at the corner deli that morning. Every day at one, he re-opened the store. Since Anne's death, he had been robbed at gunpoint twice, both times also within minutes of re-opening after lunch. Lester guessed the perpetrator must have been waiting somewhere close by, and probably knew the store's scheduled hours. He assumed all three robberies were committed by the same man, but because he wore a different hooded jacket and sunglasses each time, and because he hadn't seen who had shot Anne, he couldn't be certain. Something the man had said during the last confrontation, had convinced him further that this was, in fact, the same man who had taken Anne's life.

In his memory, Lester stared down the barrel of the revolver. The gunman stood there unwavering, fearless. Lester imagined that this was his late wife's last memory. His hands began to tremble uncontrollably as he stuffed the paper money into a brown bag.

"Hurry up!" the gunman had snapped.

"Calm down," Lester said, holding up his hand.

"Don't make me shoot again!" the gunman barked.

"Here! Here!" Lester handed over the bag.

With his free hand, the gunman snatched the bag from Lester and walked backward to the door, still pointing the gun at Lester. He crossed the threshold, pulled the door closed behind him, slid the gun into his jacket pocket and walked briskly away. Lester ran to the door and pulled it open violently. Staring out into the street, he scanned the sidewalk. He was gone. Lester ran back to the counter to the phone. He was about to call the police when he had a second thought. Instead, he pushed a button on the VCR under the counter. The tape whirred backward for a few seconds, Lester hit the play button. The image of the robber appeared on the small monitor beside the cash register.

"Calm down," he heard his voice on the recording.

"Don't make me shoot again!" the gunman repeated.

Lester hit the rewind button once more.

"Don't make me shoot again!" What did that mean? "Again?"

Anne had made Lester promise that he would not have a firearm in the store. Anne would rather just give them the money; why tempt fate by fighting back. They were insured. Lester had resignedly promised to obey the weapons ban she had imposed. However, now he was not so sure he could keep that promise.

The sound of the bell above the front door brought Lester back to the present day. He looked up to see a young woman dressed completely in black, sporting fire-engine red hair and a nose ring.

"Hi Jan," he said warmly. "Marlboro Lights?"

"Yes, please, Lester," she replied. "And can I get a Bic?"

"Any color in particular?" he asked, reaching behind him and grabbing a pink plastic lighter from a display box. Then, as if seeing the error of his ways, he turned again and grabbed a black one.

"I would have taken the pink one!" the girl said, laughing.

"Nah, it would have ruined your image." Lester punched the buttons on the register.

On seeing the total, the girl rummaged in her purse for the exact loose change and handed the coins, along with a few crumpled dollar bills, to Lester. "Thanks Lester. See you on Thursday. Wish you'd let me dye it for you."

"Nah, I'm too old for that," Lester said playfully. "I like my grey."

"Nobody likes grey, Lester," the girl said firmly. "See ya Thursday!" She turned and walked briskly out of the store. The bell signaled her exit. Lester turned to replace the pink lighter in the display. The doorbell chimed again.

"Okay! What did you forget?" he started laughing, and then the smile vanished quickly from his face. Before him stood a medium-built white male wearing a light blue hooded jacket. The hood was up concealing his hair color, while black sunglasses concealed his eyes. Lester noticed the familiar revolver in his right hand. "You again?" Lester said, not particularly surprised. He felt a lump rise in his throat.

"Fill a bag," the gunman said flatly.

"Are you the one?" Lester asked, swallowing hard.

"What?" The gunman sounded agitated.

"The one who shot my wife?" Lester leaned over the counter. "Are you?"

"Just fill the bag man!" The gunman looked over his shoulder nervously.

"I want to know!" Lester shouted. "Did you kill her?"

"If you don't hurry up I'm going to blow your head off!" The gunman was getting anxious. It was obvious he wanted out of there.

"Tell me!" Lester shouted.

"Okay, asshole. Yes! Now fill the fucking bag!" He leveled the gun at Lester's head. "Do it!" he screamed. He didn't notice a tall dark figure, also wearing a hooded jacket, step out from behind a tall stack of beer cases. The tall figure raised his hand in the gunman's direction. As the gunman turned his head with the sudden realization of his presence, the tall dark figure fired his weapon. Lester stared, as suddenly, a shower of droplets, like rubies in the sunlight, hurtled toward the glass of the front window. The gunman fell in a lifeless heap on the floor. The tall dark figure stepped forward. Reaching into his pocket with a gloved hand, he retrieved a small black card. As he walked past the body he casually dropped the card onto the dead man's chest. He turned his face in Lester's direction and nodded silently. Lester nodded back his gratitude. Without stopping, Moses quickly exited the store and walked briskly up the street.

Chapter Thirty-Six

"And you say you never saw the shooter before?" Sawyer asked, a note of disbelief in his voice.

"Never," Lester confirmed. "He was over by the beer when this guy walked in." He nodded toward the huge stainless steel refrigerator, where a CSI team were now busy dusting for fingerprints.

"Did you get a good look at his face? Was he black, white, Hispanic?"

"I didn't see his face at all. He had a hood pulled over it," Lester said flatly.

"Well, what color was he when he walked in?" Sawyer asked sarcastically. "You didn't see him walk in?"

"I told you. I was below the counter. I had just tripped over the wire to the camera. I was trying to fix it."

"Very convenient the way the camera died right before these guys walked in," Sanchez added.

"It didn't die," Lester protested. "I told you, I tripped over …"

"We know, you tripped over the wire, and ripped it out from the wall." Sanchez glanced down at the three-pronged plug still sitting in the socket, and the bare wire laying on the floor. "I thought you were fixing it. It doesn't look like you got very far."

"I was looking for my pliers on the shelf down there." Lester pointed to a cluttered shelf below the counter.

"Lucky for the perp," Sanchez said.

"Beg your pardon?" Lester looked puzzled.

"The perpetrator," Sanchez reiterated. "The guy who shot him. It was very lucky for him."

"I guess so," Lester said.

"So you say this guy worked next door?" Sawyer was squatting over the body.

"Yes. I didn't know it was him until the glasses flew off," Lester said leaning over the counter.

"The manager of the lube shop is outside," Sanchez stated. "He said one of his grease monkeys never came back from lunch break. He's ready to ID the guy whenever you are."

"So when this guy walked from the back of the shop, you still didn't see his face?" Sawyer asked, ignoring Sanchez.

"He was wearing a hood," Lester sighed, obviously tiring of the same questions.

"Must have been a pretty big hood to cover his whole face and all," Sawyer said. "What kind of hood was it? Was he wearing like a monk's hood? I know my hoodie barely covers my head."

"He was pulling it down with his hand, so I couldn't see him," Lester said.

"Which hand?" Sawyer asked.

"His left. It was the side closest to me," Lester said confidently.

"I thought you said he had the card in his left. He had to let go of the hood to get the card out of his pocket, right?" Sawyer continued.

"I forget," Lester said casually. "Maybe the card was in his right."

"So what did he do with the gun?" Sawyer kept on. "You said the gun was in his right hand."

"I don't remember," Lester said flatly. "It's a shame the camera went out, isn't it?"

"Isn't it?" Sawyer agreed. His cell phone rang in his jacket pocket. He quickly retrieved it and flipped it open. "Sawyer," he answered.

"Hi, Rick, it's Doreen, from records."

"Hey, sexy," he joked. "What you got for me?"

"Well, you were right. I found a jumper," Doreen said proudly. "Melanie Warren, nineteen-years-old, 1998, in San Antonio, Texas. She jumped from the eighth floor of the student dorm about a month before Lewis left town. The school has no records of it being related to anything academic."

"Well, they wouldn't, would they?" Sawyer said.

"But get this," Doreen continued. "Warren's mother? She has followed this guy from town to town since her daughter's death. She has camped out in front of colleges; picketed outside his apartment; made this guy's life hell. All to bring attention to the fact that her daughter named him as a rapist. Because of her, he's been released from one high school and two university jobs. Guess that's why he wasn't teaching anymore. The mother was arrested four times in four different jurisdictions. He never pressed charges, though."

"Well, he wouldn't, would he?" Sawyer said.

"But get this," Doreen continued. "She lives right here in town."

"Who does? The mother?" Sawyer suddenly sounded very interested.

"Yep!" Doreen said smugly. "Her name's Audrey Warren. She works for the state as a trauma counselor. She also runs some kind of support group for the families of victims of violent crime."

"Really?" said Sawyer. "Do you have an address?"

Chapter Thirty-Seven

"Oh my God! I'm so happy you could make it!" Meryl hugged Margo tightly. "It seems like an eternity."

"We spoke last week," Margo said with a chuckle.

"Yes, but that's not the same. Telephones don't count." She gestured toward the booth. "Tell me what you thought of the script," she said as they both sat.

"The script? Oh! The script!" Margo said. "I'll have whatever she ordered," she told an arriving waiter. "I forgot all about the script," she told her friend sheepishly. "I didn't get a chance to look at it yet."

"Are you serious?" Meryl was visibly irritated. "Margo, we've waited years for the opportunity to work together. You have to be ready by next week to read for Maury Levewitz."

"I'm sorry, Meryl," she cooed. "I'll be ready."

"Good; I'll let him know …"

Suddenly, there was a commotion across the room.

"Take it back! It's fucking cold!" Ira Morganstien's fat jowls quivered as he shook his oversized face. He was beet red with anger, a common complaint. "If she wanted cold soup she would have asked for cold soup!" He bellowed.

"It's fine Ira, honestly," Helen Morganstien whimpered.

"Shut up!" he told his petite wife. "Bring her a new one," he ordered the waiter, who hurried off with the offensive dish obediently.

"Ira Morganstein," Margo said distastefully. "He's still an arrogant asshole, I see."

"Margo!" Meryl chastised. "Shhh … someone might hear you."

"I don't give a shit," Margo replied. "He's a prick."

"Margo! What the hell?" Meryl was more than a little surprised at Margo's colorful language.

"Sorry," Margo said contritely. "I forgot who I was with."

"What does that mean?" Meryl creased her brow. "Am I that prim and proper?"

"Please, Meryl! You turned down a role because you had to take off your shirt!"

"What about you?" Meryl countered. "You turned down a role because you had to take off your makeup!"

"Hey!" Margo said with a laugh. "At least I didn't have to shave ..."

"When I say medium rare, I mean medium rare!" Ira's voice boomed again.

"I'm so sorry, sir," The waiter said nervously. "I'll bring you a new one.

"What about getting me a new fucking waiter while you're at it!" Ira bellowed.

"Certainly, sir." Margo thought she saw a flash of hatred cross the young waiter's face. He wasn't quite seasoned enough to have fully mastered that 'your shit doesn't stink' façade that is so prevalent in Beverly Hills.

"This is supposed to be a five-star restaurant. Where the hell is the manager?"

"Ira, please, keep your voice ..." His wife timidly intervened.

"I told you to shut up!" He cut her off rudely. "Who the hell are you, his fucking lawyer?"

Margo and Meryl picked at their Asian salads while they watched the pantomime that was Ira Morganstein. He was used to performing for an audience. He was one of the top producers in Hollywood. His movies were gold, but the man was a pig. Margo and Meryl both knew him well. Meryl had starred in many of his productions, while Margo knew him mainly through Jim. He had once caressed Margo's left buttock as she glided past him at an award dinner. It had taken all she had to stop Jim from beating him to death, a move that would have been career suicide, back in the day. Nowadays, they were both big enough names in the industry to get away with murder, even if it was in public.

The restaurant manager approached the Morganstein table, smiling way more than necessary. "Mr. Morganstein, I'm so sorry you had a bad experience with us today. How can I make this situation right for you?"

"Well, you can start by firing that asshole of a waiter," Morganstein ordered loudly.

"He will, too," Meryl acknowledged. "That poor kid will be pounding the streets within minutes."

"All because of that piece of shit," Margo stated.

"Sad, but there's nothing we can do about it," Meryl said taking a sip from her wine glass.

"Really? We'll see about that!"

Margo stood up. She threw her napkin into the center of the table and strode in the direction of Morganstein's table. As she neared the table, he looked up.

"Margo Priestley?" he said with a lecherous smile. "How the hell are ..."

Margo struck him hard over the head with the wine bottle she had grabbed from the bucket beside him. He fell forward, face down in the fresh steak that had just been delivered. Helen Morganstein let out a scream.

"Margo!" Meryl called from the table behind her. "Margo!"

Blood oozed from the head wound she had created. Margo stared in wonder at her own handiwork. *Serves him right, cantankerous bastard!,* she thought.

"Margo!" Meryl called frantically. "Are you even listening to a word I'm saying?"

Margo looked across the table at her friend in confusion. She looked over at the Morganstein table. There was Ira, cutting into a new steak, still complaining, head intact.

"Oh, I'm sorry," she said. "I was somewhere else for a moment." She reached across the table and grabbed the wine bottle in front of her. "I think I've been watching too much television," she said, refilling her glass.

The rest of their lunch was pretty much undisturbed, apart from the occasional defamatory remark thrown by Ira at his mild-mannered spouse. Margo opened her purse and retrieved her wallet.

"No need for that, Ms. Priestley. It was my pleasure. Have a wonderful day, ladies." The manager beamed at them.

"Thank you, Stephan." Margo nodded and placed a hundred-dollar bill in the center of the table. She had a habit of over-tipping. She took a business card from inside her wallet and slipped it into her jacket pocket. "Are you ready?" she asked Meryl, placing the strap of her bag over her shoulder.

"Yes," Meryl answered. "Thank you for a lovely lunch."

"No, let's thank Ira," Margo said with a smile.

"What?" Meryl asked nervously. "Margo? Wait, what are you doing?"

Margo threw her napkin into the center of the table and strode in the direction of Morganstein's table. As she neared the table, he looked up. This time when he opened his mouth to speak he was cut short by ice water violently thrown in his face. He gasped to get his breath, as he tried to get up from his seat.

"If you don't sit down and shut your fat mouth I will have both your fucking legs broken." Margo said calmly, leaning into his face. Something about her eyes must have told him she was serious, so he lowered himself quietly back into his seat. She reached into her jacket pocket and took out the card she had placed there a short while ago. She thrust it into Helen Morganstein's hand. "This is my divorce lawyer," she said abruptly. "I got the kid, the house, his Lamborghini, and a huge check. Do yourself a favor, call him." With that, she strode toward the front door, Meryl in tow.

Chapter Thirty-Eight

Sawyer walked into the interrogation room, a broad smile on his face. Sanchez followed close behind, a noticeable scowl on his.

"Hi, Audrey! I'm Detective Sawyer," he boomed. "This is my partner, Detective Sanchez. Thanks for coming in to talk with us." He leaned forward with an outstretched hand. With his other hand he nonchalantly pushed the record button on a large digital recorder. "Do you have any idea why we asked you here today, Audrey?"

"Oh, I think so," Audrey said, smiling as she shook his hand. She glanced over at Sanchez, now seated on a wooden chair in the corner. "Judging by Grumpy over here, you must be the good cop." Sanchez scowled harder.

"So why do you think you're here?" Sawyer asked taking the seat across from Audrey.

"Well, probably because you think I killed Arthur Lewis," Audrey said bluntly.

"Why would I think that, Audrey?" Sawyer put his right elbow on the table and rested his chin on his palm.

"Probably because nobody wanted to see him dead more than me," Audrey said without emotion.

"Why is that?" Sawyer asked innocently.

"Well, I'm assuming you already know, or I wouldn't be sitting here." Audrey folded her arms.

"When did you last see Arthur Lewis alive?" Sanchez asked sternly from the corner.

"Alive?" Audrey frowned. "Are you insinuating I have seen him in any other condition?"

"When did you last see him?" Sanchez rephrased the question.

"About three years ago." She offered nothing more.

"Would you like to elaborate on that?" Sawyer asked with his good cop smile.

"Sure. I got a tip from a friend that he was going for an interview for a science teacher position at one of the local high schools. I made a point of being there when he arrived. I had a nice sign made up that said 'Student Killer'." She smiled wickedly. "He didn't get the job."

"And that was the last time you saw him?" Sanchez asked.

"Yes," she answered flatly.

"Where were you on the morning of August ninth?" Sanchez' eyebrows drew closer together.

"At what time?" she asked.

"From midnight to noon." Sanchez did not appreciate her attitude.

"Bed, shower, breakfast, whale-watching; in that order." Her facial expressions were unchanging.

"What do mean, whale-watching?" Sanchez asked.

"I was watching whales," she replied. "You know, big mammals — swim about in the ocean?"

"Where was this?" Sanchez asked.

"In Oregon. I was there for a week of seminars, with a couple of hundred other people. I didn't have any other commitments, so I stayed for the weekend after the seminars finished and returned on the Tuesday morning." She stared coolly across at Sanchez.

"Can anyone corroborate your story?" Sanchez looked a little perturbed.

"Let's see. There's the hotel staff, the boat crew, the guy I was sleeping with the whole week I was up there." She shrugged her shoulders. "Apart from them, nobody really."

"Do you ever talk about Melanie to the people you counsel?" Sawyer asked.

"Why would I do that? I'm there to counsel them." She leaned forward in her chair. "Believe me, Detective Sawyer, I talked to anyone and everyone about my daughter and Lewis for a long time. Nobody would listen to me. So I did my best to make sure he couldn't hurt anyone else's child. I don't need to bring it up anymore, especially at one of my support meetings. I've dealt with my issues."

"So you never mentioned it to anyone in the group?" Sanchez pressed.

"Absolutely not," Audrey insisted.

"Can you think of anyone who might want to avenge Melanie's death for you? Perhaps someone who can sympathize with your situation? Maybe someone who might care about you personally?" Sawyer attempted to rephrase the question. "Maybe someone in the group who could have heard about Melanie?"

"I told you, I don't talk about me. I'm there to listen to them."

"Would you be willing to give us a list of the people in the group?" Sawyer asked.

"No," she replied.

"You know we can subpoena a court order to release those records if we have to." Sanchez sounded smug.

"All they give me is an attendance sheet of the people who are required, either by law, or for medical reasons, to attend. Most of them are there voluntarily. They come and go as they feel the need. I don't have any records on these people. You'd have to go through the counseling center for that kind of information, but there are confidentiality laws, as you well know. So I guess all I can say is," she turned to Sanchez, "subpoena away."

Chapter Thirty-Nine

Marcus Jamieson was a handsome young man. His clean-cut, all-American features enhanced his large, muscular physique. He had been captain of his high school football team and had played all of his college years. He had been the choice of every cheerleader he had ever met; using his good looks to his advantage many times. He was the apple of his mother's eye and a chip off his father's old block. Well, until he told them he was gay. He still called Mom now and again, but sadly, only when he knew his father wouldn't be there.

"Do you want tacos or should I make steak salad?" he asked, looking into the refrigerated counter.

"I don't know," Alex answered. "Where are you? Is there any fish?"

"No. I'm at Chico's Market."

"Ew! I don't know why you go there. It's in such a bad area," Alex said. "Why do you always go there?"

"It's on the way home," Marcus countered, "and I like their carne asada. Do you want tacos?"

"Whatever. I'll be here for a while yet," he told his significant other. He added a little more blood to the scar that ran the length of the severed head on his bench. "I still have to work on a few more prosthetic scars for the hatchet scene. Call me when you've decided what you're going to poison me with."

"Okay, bitch!" Marcus closed the phone smiling. If he was going to be that way about it, it would definitely be the carne asada. There was nothing wrong with the food here. They had gotten sick only that one time, and there was no way of proving that the meat from Chico's was to blame. He filled his basket with his recipe's ingredients and headed for the checkout. A man with tattoos and a red bandana was leaning against the counter. He eyed the bulge in Marcus' back pocket. Not seeming to notice, Marcus pulled his wallet from the pocket and flicked through the hundred dollar bills, looking for a twenty. The man in the bandana nodded to another similarly-dressed man who was apparently looking for something in the refrigerator.

"Carne asada!" Marcus declared into the phone as he exited the store.

"Ew!" Alex moaned.

"I'll let you have the bathroom first," Marcus joked. "I thought you liked my ... Hang on a minute. There are three guys following me."

"Oh, my God!" Alex said in a panic. "Give them whatever they want, Marcus!"

"Yeah, right. Like that's gonna happen." Marcus sounded annoyed. "Excuse me?" He said to someone Alex couldn't see.

"Marcus, what's going on? Just give them your wallet," Alex said, trying hard to keep the panic from his voice.

"I'm sorry! You want what?" Marcus said loudly. "Are you serious?"

"Marcus, just give it to them!" Alex yelled into the phone. "Did you hear me? Marcus? ... Marcus? ... MARCUS!!!!"

~

Alex stood as Margo approached the table. His genuine smile grew wider as she drew nearer. "Oh, my God! You look fantastic!" He opened his arms wide. "I've missed you so much," he said, wrapping his arms around her tightly.

"I've missed you, too!" Margo crooned. They held each other close for almost a minute before sitting. Both with tears in their eyes.

"I haven't seen you since the funeral," Alex said flatly. "Oh, my God! How long has it been?"

"Eight months," Margo answered. "Time flies when you're having fun."

"Eight months? I'm sorry, Margo. I guess I've just been trying to stay busy, you know? I try to keep my mind occupied, if you know what I mean. Oh, I'm sorry; of course you do." He smiled lamely and rolled his eyes. "I think I might have a date this weekend."

"Oh, honey, I'm so pleased. It's been a year. You know Marcus would be happy." She squeezed his hand affectionately. "Do I know him?" She asked genuinely interested.

"No, he's a stunt guy at the studio. At least he'll understand the hours I have to put in. Marcus was always such a pain in the ass about my working so late." He threw his hands up in the air. "I don't know if I can love someone else," he said softly, "but I'd like to try."

Margo took his hand in hers and rubbed it softly. "You can love, Alex," she said tenderly. "It's what you do best."

"So, what about you? Are we over Jim yet?" He raised his eyebrows. Margo did not answer. "I didn't think so. We'll just have to get rid of the frog. Let me know if you need my help."

"Well, actually, I do need your help, but not with the frog." Margo paused when the waitress brought a bottle of Chardonnay Alex had ordered.

"I hope you don't mind," he said. "I was in the mood for something light."

"You read my mind," Margo said picking up the menu. "I know what I'm having. They have great Dover sole here." She put down the menu and picked up her glass. "Mmm, that's good," she said after taking a sip.

"Ooh, that sounds good. I'll have the sole, too," he told the waitress. "And can you bring some calamari?" he asked. The waitress left, smiling and nodding.

"So what do you need, darling?" He clasped his hands together. "Anything."

"Anything?" she repeated.

"What is it, Margo? What's going on?" His curiosity was piqued.

Margo reached her hand into her pocket. Looking around to see no one was watching, she slid a small card face down across the table. She took a sip from her glass. "I'm taking a huge leap of faith here," she said softly. She removed her hand from atop the card.

Alex turned over the business card. He'd seen the news. He'd read the papers. He recognized the card immediately. "Oh, my God, Margo. It's you?"

"I'll understand if you don't want to get involved," she whispered. "I only ask that you don't give me away. Not yet anyway. I still have something I have to do."

"Give you away? Are you out of your mind? After what happened to Marcus?" A solitary tear ran down his cheek. "I am so proud of you, Margo Priestley, and I'm honored that you deem me worthy of involvement. If I can do anything at all, just ask."

"Oh, you can," she smiled. "And I will." She pressed a small silver lapel pin into his hand.

Chapter Forty

Simon looked up when the cell door slid open. He wasn't expecting to see anyone today. His lawyer wasn't coming until tomorrow and his parents had just left. He pushed himself back against the wall. He was scared, extremely scared. The county jail was full to capacity, and so he was being held here at the penitentiary until other accommodations could be found for him and eight other young men awaiting trial. Although he was supposed to be sequestered from the other inmates he had run across a few of them during his short incarceration. He had witnessed first-hand the loathing the other prisoners felt for him. The gash on his right cheek was a constant reminder. The handmade shank had intentionally been aimed for his eye, but the guard had caught sight of it at the last moment and managed to grab the assailant before he could make contact. Still, he had managed to lash out violently, leaving his mark on Simon's delicate features. Simon wondered later whether or not the guard had actually known about the proposed attack beforehand.

Simon's good looks had not gone unnoticed. Many times a day those inmates with liberty to walk around would stop outside his cell to tell him of their desire to be his best friend on the inside. Some were more blunt than others, but all had made it blatantly clear that when he was eventually released into the general population, he was going to have lots of company. His lawyer was fighting feverishly to have him moved to another location, but the courts were not as sympathetic to his plight as they might have been to another's.

The tall black prisoner walked backward into the cell. One guard bent down to remove the shackles from his feet, while the other held a nightstick threateningly. When the guard stood up unscathed, the tall black prisoner held up his shackled hands to be freed. The guard unlocked them, and fastened them back securely onto his belt.

"Okay, top bunk!" He told the new addition to Simon's humble abode.

The tall black prisoner turned around. Simon's attention was immediately drawn to his face. A long deep scar ran the length of his face from the center of his forehead through his left eyebrow to the jaw line just below his left ear. The scar was almost a half inch wide in parts, and Simon wondered what kind of weapon could have caused it. He had to have been cut right to the bone. The prisoner saw Simon's expression.

"You know me?" he asked in deep voice. Simon shook his head rapidly to indicate that he did not.

"So what the fuck you looking at?"

Simon quickly averted his attention back to the word-search puzzle he had been preoccupied with earlier. The guard slid the door back in place loudly.

"Play nice, Isaiah," he said laughing. The other guard mumbled something under his breath, and the two laughed again, before walking away leaving the two strangers to become acquainted.

"You smoke?" Isaiah asked. Simon shook his head. "Good. 'cause I hate that shit."

"You a faggot?" Isaiah stared at him. Again Simon shook his head. "Good. 'cause I ain't into that shit, either. I don't want to have to worry where the fuck you are at night." Simon looked back at his puzzle. "You a fuckin' mute?"

"No," Simon answered shakily.

Isaiah moved toward him. Simon stared up at his colossal frame, fear in his eyes. Isaiah placed one foot on Simon's bed and pulled himself up onto the top bunk. The mattress bowed down above Simon's head. It appeared that the conversation was over. Simon let out a small sigh of relief.

"I don't want nobody watching me piss," the voice from the top bunk said. "When I use the john, you look the other way. I'll do the same for you. Get it?"

"Yes," Simon answered sheepishly.

It was funny. For the first time since he arrived, Simon actually felt at ease. Isaiah was one scary looking son-of-a-bitch, but he had let Simon know immediately that he didn't want anything from him, and that he expected a certain level of respect between the two. This was the best Simon could have hoped for inside. Isaiah did not want to be close friends and apparently held no animosity toward him. Light snoring came from the bunk above. Isaiah felt secure enough to fall asleep, and why shouldn't he? Simon was no threat to him. Hell, Isaiah looked as though he could beat the crap out of Simon with his eyes closed, and Simon had absolutely no intention of antagonizing him. He lay down on his bunk and closed his eyes. Maybe things would be better for him now. Perhaps the other inmates would not be so quick to stop by his cell with their lewd remarks and vicious threats. Not with Isaiah standing right there beside him. He hoped not anyway. He drifted off into what was probably his first peaceful sleep since his arrest.

"Ice!" a whispered voice came from outside the bars of the cell. Simon looked up to see a Hispanic male dressed in an over-sized orange jumpsuit holding a large mop. He wore a brightly-colored bandana on his head, which sat low on his forehead, almost covering his eyes. Simon could see tattoos from his neck down. They completely covered his hands and a solitary tattooed-teardrop sat below his left eye.

"Ice," the man hissed through the bars again.

"My name's not Ice; it's Isaiah. How many times I gotta fucking tell you?" Isaiah jumped down from the bunk.

"Relax, man! I just came to tell you we're still on for tonight."

"Shh!" Isaiah looked over at Simon. Simon looked away quickly. "Tonight? No way, Lopez; they're watchin'."

"They're not gonna 'spect it tonight. They think they caught you 'tempting a break. They're not gonna 'spect you to try again so soon. It's the perfect time. dude." Lopez was talking barely loud enough for Simon to hear.

"Shit! I don't know, man." Isaiah shook his head.

"The car's in place, dude," Lopez said. "We've still got the key! You already paid for this man."

"But tonight?" Isaiah questioned.

"Dude, we planned this. It's all set up." Lopez looked over his shoulder and began mopping. He shuffled forward, slowly mopping in front of the bars. "Dude, you got nothing to lose. If you don't go tonight they'll move you to the max house tomorrow. Once you get on death row, you don't get another chance. You better be ready, dude. It's tonight, man." He moved away from the cell.

Isaiah turned slowly and headed back toward the bunks. Simon pretended to be asleep. Isaiah stopped directly in front of him, his eyes piercing through the darkness until Simon could feel his stare forcing him to open his eyes. He looked up at Isaiah's angry expression.

"You didn't hear a damn thing. You got me? It would be real fucking stupid to cross me, white boy." Placing his foot on Simon's bed, he prepared to send himself aloft.

"Isaiah?" Simon's voice was almost a whisper.

"What?" Isaiah sounded annoyed.

"Please ... I ... I ... Will you take me with you?"

Chapter Forty-One

"So they just walked out of here? How the hell does that happen?" Rick Sawyer stared in disbelief at the images being displayed on the many monitors of the prison surveillance room. "I mean look at this; they're just tip-toeing right on out of here."

"Someone hit the surveillance monitor guard from behind," the prison warden explained.

"How did they get in the room?" Sawyer asked. "It's supposed to be locked at all times."

"What exactly are you implying?" the Warden asked indignantly.

"I'm not implying anything. I'm just wondering. How many keys are there to this room, and how easy would it be to get hold of one to copy?"

"I believe there are two. One that is kept in this room at all times, and another that is signed out daily to whoever has the shift on that day." The warden pointed to a lock box mounted on the wall. The box had a numeric keypad at the bottom. "All guards with access to this room have their own code to open the box. That way we can track the individuals who have opened it. There is no reason to open this box unless the other key is gone for some reason. Both keys have been accounted for, Detective Sawyer. The injured guard had his key on his belt, and nobody has opened this box in over a month."

"So why was it opened a month ago?"

"I don't know. Let's check the log." The warden walked over to a small cabinet, which sat below the lock box. In it were the daily signatures of the guards who had had duty in the surveillance room over the last six months. "The front of the book holds the signatures for the roaming key; the back is for the lock box. It's like a double tally. The signature has to match the code," he said flicking to the last few pages of the log. "It says here the last time it was opened was for regular scheduled maintenance."

"How often does that happen?" Sawyer queried.

"Every three months." He checked the book again. "Yep! Three months to the day."

"So it appears there is either a third key knocking around, or the guard on duty let his assailant in," Sawyer presumed.

"I would have to go with the third key theory," the Warden agreed. "The guard was slumped over the monitors. He never left his seat."

"Unless," Sawyer suggested, "it was staged to look that way."

"Again, Detective Sawyer, what exactly are you implying?" The Warden, although not overly agitated, seemed somewhat displeased with Sawyer's assumptions.

"Something stinks here," he said bluntly. "Look at the way these three are just moseying down the corridors. Nobody stops them. Look, look at this guard! They duck into a doorway, and he passes within inches of them."

"He obviously didn't know they were there," the Warden said, sounding more than a little perturbed.

"Or did he?" Sawyer continued. "In every camera shot, we see Fulton's face clearly. I can see the freckles on his face."

"And your point is?"

"My point is, we never get a look at the other two inmates. Their faces are always angled away from the cameras like they know exactly where they are," Sawyer exclaimed excitedly. "See, I can read the number on Fulton's uniform without even trying, but not the other two; why?"

"Well this one is walking backward most of the time," the warden offered.

"Why?" Sawyer asked. "Why is he doing that?"

"I'm assuming it's so one of them is watching either direction at all times," the warden proposed.

"Maybe," Sawyer agreed somewhat. "But we never get to see the other guy's face either. The most we can tell is he's a heavily-tattooed Hispanic male. Kind of sums up a third of the inmates, doesn't it? Have you noticed how he casually draped the bandana over his left shoulder so we can't read his number?"

"Well, we have pictures of his tattoos, and we know he walks with a limp on his right side," the warden said positively. "It shouldn't be too long before we can identify him. All identifying marks are logged on a monthly basis, especially tattoos on the face and head, and this guy has tattoos all over his scalp."

"That's another thing. Why would he be so careful to cover up his number, but show us his tattoos. He blatantly bares the top of his head to the camera all the time, but he never looks up once."

"Well most of the inmates know where the cameras are after they've been here a few weeks. It's the first thing they learn," the warden offered. "Perhaps he wears the bandana most of the time and figures we won't recognize the tattoos."

"Or maybe he doesn't have any tattoos. Maybe he's not an inmate," Sawyer said. "When will we have that number?"

"We should have it anytime in the next thirty minutes. The place is on lockdown, and I have four teams doing a head count."

"I think you'll find you only have one inmate missing: Fulton." Sawyer said. "Someone went to great lengths to get this kid out of here, and I don't know who, or why, yet. But I have my suspicions."

Chapter Forty-Two

Sawyer was a little surprised when the front door was opened by Margo Priestley personally. She looked at him with a puzzled expression.

"Detective Sawyer? Come in." She held open the door, and gestured graciously for him to enter.

"No housekeeper today?" he asked casually. He stepped into the spacious entry way.

"No. I'm afraid I'm self-sufficient for a little while longer. Carla went to visit her daughter in San Francisco. In fact, she should be arriving back in town in about half an hour." she said, looking at her watch. She showed him into the den where she had been perhaps a little less than civil to him on his last visit. Still, he could understand that.

"Would you like something to drink?" she offered. "I should warn you, I've been told my coffee leaves a lot to be desired." She smiled warmly. What a difference a few months can make. He very nearly liked her today. Margo pointed to one of the couches and Sawyer took a seat, obediently. She sat opposite him on a large overstuffed armchair.

"No, thank you; I don't want to put you to any trouble." He returned the smile. "I actually wanted to ask you a couple of questions, and let you know about the latest developments in the case."

"Questions?" Margo raised her eyebrows. "About Cassi?"

"No, actually." He reached into his inside jacket pocket for a small notepad. "Would you by any chance know of your whereabouts on June 12th?" he asked, casually flicking through the pages.

"June 12th?" Margo asked astonished. "Detective Sawyer, I couldn't tell you where I was yesterday! Can you be a little more specific? Was it a weekday? Daytime, nighttime?" She shrugged her shoulders.

"Roughly eleven p.m. on a Friday night," Sawyer said without emotion. "A black BMW, licensed to you, plate number …"

"Black BMW?" Margo interrupted. "In June? I lost my BMW back in March," Margo informed him.

"It was stolen?" Sawyer assumed.

"No. I had a fire in the garage; something to do with the electrical wiring."

"The wiring in the car?" he asked.

"No, in the garage," Margo replied. "I don't remember exactly, but I think mice chewed through some wires. I have the paperwork somewhere." She walked over to a large mahogany desk. After rifling through the filing cabinet for a few minutes she pulled out a manila folder. "I think it's in here," she said, handing him the paperwork.

"Looks like someone got hold of your license plate," Sawyer said while scanning the documents, "probably from the scrap yard or the towing company."

"Oh, my! Someone used my plates? Was it for a robbery?" Margo sounded distressed.

"Vehicular homicide," Sawyer said flatly. "The car was probably stolen. They just used your plate to make it street legal." He closed the folder. "Can I take this and make copies?"

"Sure," she shrugged. "I feel terrible that my plate could have been used to hurt someone."

"Kill someone," Sawyer corrected her.

"So you said there are some developments in the case." Margo calmly changed the subject. "What developments? Did he change his plea?"

"No," he answered.

"Have they settled on a court date? Oh, my God!" she gasped, sitting down. "I'm not ready for this. I don't think any of us are. Does Jim know yet?"

"Ms. Priestley, they haven't come up with a court date yet. That's not what I wanted to tell you." Margo's brows creased. He continued, "Simon Fulton is no longer in custody."

"What? Are you serious? Don't tell me they granted him bail!" She raced over to the telephone and started dialing.

"Ms. Priestley," Sawyer said firmly. "Who are you calling?"

"My lawyer! He's got to stop this!" Her breathing was becoming erratic. Sawyer crossed the room and calmly put his finger on the disconnect button.

"Ms. Priestley, that won't do any good." He took the receiver out of her hand and placed it back in the cradle. "Simon Fulton wasn't released; he escaped."

"How?" she demanded. Sawyer watched as her face gradually turned from its natural creamy color to a deep red. "Where is he?' she screamed.

"He escaped during the early hours of the morning," Sawyer explained.

"How?" she shouted. "How did he escape? He was in a goddamn prison for God's sake." Her face was contorted into an evil grimace.

"It appears he had a little help," Sawyer didn't want to give up too much information.

"A little help?!" Margo wailed. "What the hell do you mean, he had a little help?!" Suddenly her face was inches from his own. "Find him! Find him!" she screamed.

Just then the front door opened. Carla's face peered around it. On hearing the commotion inside she flung the door wide open to reveal Jim close behind her. She hurriedly walked inside.

"Margo, what is it?" She called, rushing to her side. Margo was holding the lapels of Sawyer's jacket tightly in her hands, shaking him frantically. "Margo! What's going on?"

Jim was there, all at once, pulling her off Sawyer. He managed to free her hands from the coat and directed her to the couch. She collapsed into it, sobbing uncontrollably. Carla sat beside her, holding her as though she were a small child.

"What the hell happened?" Jim snapped at Sawyer. "What did you say to her?"

"I told her Fulton had escaped from prison," Sawyer repeated.

"What?! When?" Jim yelled.

"Last night," Sawyer answered. "I didn't think she'd take it so badly."

"How the hell did you expect her to take it?" He looked back over at Margo. "From now on you speak to me first!" he ordered.

"Hey, I'm sorry. I didn't mean to cause her this kind of distress." Sawyer looked over at the couch. He sighed heavily. He hated this part of the job. He hated that sometimes he had to hurt the innocent to get to the truth. "I'll let myself out," he added dejectedly.

Margo focused on Sawyer through the stream of tears. She watched as Jim escorted him to the door. Who the hell did he think he was dealing with? Did he really think he was going to catch her off guard? She could lie through her teeth and not bat an eyelid. She could look him straight in the eye and he would never know what was truly going on inside. She was a master of deception. She was a goddamn professional. She was an Oscar-winning actress for God's sake.

Chapter Forty-Three

Sawyer pulled at the knot in his tie until it sat loosely in the center of his chest. He unfastened the two top buttons of his shirt, leaned back in his seat, closed his eyes, and sighed loudly. He rubbed his tired eyes. This case was really starting to piss him off. He retrieved his keys from his jacket pocket and started up the car. He looked back at Margo Priestley's palatial home in the rear view mirror. *Well that went fucking well Rick,* he thought sullenly. He had really had her pegged as the main suspect in Fulton's disappearance, but now he was not so sure. Sawyer was one hell of a good judge of character, normally. He had seen through so many facades put up by so many criminals, in the past. Facades that had family members, the police, and even judges fooled, but not Rick Sawyer. He had an uncanny acumen for being able to read people. An ability to see through them. The mother who had kept the body of her three year old in a freezer for over a year. The boy who had denied all knowledge of his missing girlfriend's whereabouts, until she had been found in a shallow grave, in his parents' back yard. The cop who had heroically shot and killed the fatal attacker of a young woman, but was then later proved to be the murderer of both, in a tragic love triangle. Sawyer had seen through them all. Small telltale signs, in their eyes, their voices, or their mannerisms, that had told him to keep questioning, keep examining, keep digging. He had really believed that Priestley was in on the prison break, but the last fifteen minutes had persuaded him otherwise. There had been genuine panic in her eyes, and distress that her daughter's murderer was on the loose. He could tell true anguish when he saw it. Shame, he thought he was close to wrapping this one up. He needed more time to work on that damn vigilante murders case. He really needed to close that one, especially since the trail had gone cold on the Hendrix case.

It had been over a year since a cop had been murdered in the Los Angeles area. Well, murdered by the 'Copinator' as he was affectionately known by the press. It was officially the Hendrix case, named after the first officer murdered. There had been four in all. Mark Hendrix, a career police officer, had been shot in the back of the head, execution style at the side of his cruiser, two weeks after the New Year. Three months later on the same date, the fifteenth, Ken Wilson, a California Highway motorcycle cop, was found stabbed to death in his apartment. The next victim was Police Chief, Joe Hyler, who was found six months later, again on the fifteenth, dead from asphyxiation. The attacker had apparently laid in wait in Hyler's own car, strangling him with a piece of heavy nylon cord, wrapped around a plastic bag, which covered Hyler's head.

Sawyer had studied and earned a degree in psychology at Boston University, with a view to becoming a child guidance counselor, after seeing endless cases of domestic violence during his two years as a uniformed patrol officer. He had instead, opted to remain in law enforcement, as a police profiler. With eight years in the N.Y.P.D to his credit, and a strong reputation for accuracy in the field of profiling, he was offered a position by the L.A.P.D, as a homicide detective working on the Hendrix case. Much to Angela's chagrin, they left their native New York, and Sawyer arrived in Los Angeles ready to take on the case.

Sawyer Started work in LA on the eighth, in full anticipation of a murder occurring on the fifteenth. He was not disappointed. True to schedule, Detective Rose Dawson was found on January fifteenth, in a wooded area south of LA. She had been completely relieved of her skin, field dressed like a deer. This was, by far, the most heinous crime committed thus far. Other law enforcement officers had immediately blamed the elevated level of brutality on the widely publicized arrival of the New York profiler. Even Sawyer had realized that the various segments in the news about him might provoke a more violent reaction from the killer. He understood completely the resentment felt for him by his co-workers, but it did not help him in his endeavors to catch the culprit. With his superior's permission he enlisted the help of his former partner, Joe Sanchez, who flew out from New York as soon as he received the call. Right now Sawyer needed someone who felt a degree of loyalty toward him, and that appeared to be in short supply right now. Sadly, even with his trusted partner working beside him, Sawyer was at a dead end. It was then that he came up with the idea to provoke the murderer into one more attack, only this time Sawyer would be the target.

"It is my belief ," he told reporters, "that we are dealing, not only with a psychotic murderer, but also a sexual deviant. There was evidence of sexual perverseness at each crime scene, which leads me to believe the culprit was sexually abused as a child, by either one, or both of his parents. He is probably abusing weaker members of his family too, most likely small children. This is a person who needs to dominate. He probably has a Napoleon complex." In actual fact, Sawyer believed none of this. This killer was a shrewd, intelligent, and calculating factor, in this equation. There had been absolutely no sexual abuse in any of the cases. This was a ploy, that would hopefully enrage the murderer into acting irrationally, resulting in him making the mistake that would result in his demise. Sawyer's only hope was to humiliate, and defame him into retaliating directly against Sawyer. Hopefully before the murderer reaped his revenge on Sawyer, they would catch him. Sawyer knew it would work, only how long it would take was anybody's guess.

Sawyer did not have to wait too long for that retaliation. It occurred on April 15th, exactly three months after Dawson's death. Sadly though, it resulted in the grisly death of an innocent man. Due to a recent fender bender in his own car, Sawyer was riding shotgun with his partner Sanchez, when they received an APB that a body had been discovered at the back of a downtown body shop. Upon his arrival at the scene, Sawyer immediately realized that he, himself, had been the target. A man approximately Sawyer's height and build, lay face down beside a grey Crown Victoria. *His* grey Crown Victoria. He recognized the victim as the young man who had been dropped at his home earlier that morning dressed in a tee shirt and jeans. Sawyer had talked with him inside the garage, before the man backed the car out and drove it to the shop. Apparently, someone else had been watching. Someone who followed, who they assumed was Sawyer, to the alley at the back of the repair shop. Apparently it was customary for customers to drive in this way, this early in the morning, before the shop was even open. So the young man must not have thought anything of another car pulling in, and probably did not even look over his shoulder when someone walked up behind him. Hopefully the first blow, from whatever the weapon was, had rendered him unconscious, because there had been many,

many blows. Enough to leave the skull completely crushed, the face totally beyond recognition. Whoever did this was angry, really angry, but not at this guy. Whoever did this wanted Sawyer, bad. Using this knowledge, another interview was given, in order to inform the murderer that he had indeed failed in his attempt to kill Sawyer. That was a year ago. There had been no more cop killings, and the surveillance on Sawyer and his home had been dropped, as there was apparently, no longer the need. The killer had vanished and the case had gone cold.

Sawyer shook the thought from his head, just in time to notice the elderly Asian man, who had suddenly stepped out in front of him, pushing a shopping cart full of groceries. Sawyer slammed his foot hard on the brake pedal. The car screeched to a halt just inches from the elderly man who was now shaking his fist furiously at Sawyer, while feverishly shouting insults in his native tongue. He spat on the hood of Sawyer's car. Sawyer looked up to see the light was red, and the walks sign was just starting to flash, indicating that the driver was definitely in the wrong.

"Shit!" Sawyer exhaled loudly. "I'm sorry!" He called to the Asian man who was now walking rapidly to beat the light. He put the car in park and sat back shaking. *God that was close!* A horn sounded. A car had pulled up behind him. Sawyer looked up at the rear view mirror and mouthed the words, "Pull around me." He wound down the window and signaled with his hand for the car to pass him. The car behind sounded his horn again, longer and louder this time. "Pull around me asshole!" Sawyer spat into the mirror, still gesturing with his hand. The honking continued, and was now chorused by the car behind the car behind. Sawyer reached down and grabbed a blue dome from beneath his dash. Reaching out the window he slammed the magnetic base against the roof of his car. The blue dome began to flash. The honking ceased immediately. "Yeah that's right!" he yelled out the window at the cars, as they pulled slowly around him.

Sawyer cupped his hands over his face and sighed heavily. He rubbed his eyes and then perused the damage caused by his sudden stop. The entire contents of his passenger seat, his makeshift desk, had crashed to the floor of the car. *Shit!* His laptop, His digital camera, notepads, Angela's DVDs. *Shit!* he thought again, looking at his watch, it was two-fifty. He was supposed to drop them off this morning, they were due back before noon. Now he would have to go inside the store, and pay the late fee before Angela found out. That killed him, especially when Angela and her stupid teacher friends kept watching these old crap movies. *Classic my ass.* What did she have this week? He reached down and scooped up two cases. "To Kill a Mocking Bird" *That's not too bad.* He flipped the back disc to the front. "Faces of Eve" *Are you fucking kidding me?* Angie had made him watch that with her years ago, about some woman with multiple personalities. *What a load of...... A woman with multiple personalities.* "Shit!" Sawyer beat the steering wheel hard with his clenched fist. "She's a fucking actress, you idiot!" he scolded himself.

Chapter Forty-Four

Isaiah traced the angry-looking scar that ran the length of his face with his fingertips. It aged him immensely, he thought. It was a hideous-looking thing, the kind of scar that led to speculation of how it was procured. A sure sign that the owner had led an odious life. He would be glad when it was gone. Carefully he looked under his ear for the point where the latex ended, but couldn't see it. He felt for it with his fingertips. Shit! He couldn't feel a thing. Not with this stuff on his hands, anyway. He stared at the inside of his wrist for a seam. Hah, he found it! He picked at the edge until it lifted up enough to grab between his thumb and forefinger. Slowly he began to peel back the layer of latex from his palm. He made short gasps through puckered lips.

"Stings like a son of a bitch, don't it?" Raul asked smiling. "Wait till you pull the shit off your face. You've got hairs there."

"Quit winding him up!" Alex said laughing. "Pull it off fast, Moses; it won't hurt as much."

"I can't do it!" Moses answered timidly.

"Come here!" Alex said, rolling his eyes. He quickly ripped the latex of Moses' palm.

"Shit!" Moses complained loudly. "That stings, man!"

"Told ya!" Raul said elatedly.

"What a big baby!" Alex sighed, shaking his head. "Give me the other hand."

"You didn't tell me this stuff was gonna hurt comin' off!" Moses whined.

"You didn't ask," Alex said in his defense. "Would you rather have left prints behind?"

"No," Moses replied, pouting. "Ow!" He yelled as Alex ripped the latex off the other hand. "Shit! You ain't touching my goddamn head!"

"Fine," Alex said smugly. "Please yourself. The longer it's on there the stronger the bond." He sashayed out of the bathroom. "Make sure you pull it off *real slow*," he called over his shoulder.

Chapter Forty-Five

The sudden rush of cold water hitting his face made Simon Fulton gasp for air. The images before him were blurry and a strange metallic taste filled his mouth, a side effect of his chloroform-induced sleep. Groggily, he attempted to wipe the water from his face, only to find his hands were bound at the wrists and secured to a large metal ring in the concrete floor before him. Looking down, he noticed he was naked. His eyes wandered the room, gradually becoming more focused. It was a large room, kind of institutional in appearance. The floor was concrete with a line of large metal rings down the center of it. The ceiling played host to a collection of fluorescent light strips, which made his head spin as he looked at them. He quickly averted his attention to the walls, painted in a cream-colored semi-gloss paint. He noticed there were no windows, just a solitary, heavy door with a lone, wire-reinforced window at eye level. There were more metal rings, evenly spaced around the room, about four feet up each wall but one, on which was situated a huge mirror that practically ran its full length. In one corner he noticed what appeared to be a large room, or cell with bars. A group of people stood before it, a couple of them leaning up against the bars, as if waiting for something.

"This is the old eighteenth precinct," A woman's voice said from across the room. "It's slated for demolition at the end of the month. It's going to be a shopping center," she said flatly. Beside her stood a tall black man holding an empty bucket. "This was the holding room. It's situated in the center of the building and was made soundproof so that the drunks couldn't disturb the rest of the building. The lights in this room can't be seen from the street. Nobody on the outside knows we're here. We won't be disturbed. Kind of like that little secluded clearing where you took my daughter."

For the first time, Margo saw a sincere display of emotion on Fulton's face. It was a look of terror. "Are you going to kill me?" he gasped.

"Oh yes," Margo replied nonchalantly, walking toward him. "But not before we've had some fun. What's the matter? You like to have fun, don't you?" She smiled with expressionless eyes.

Fulton looked frantically around the room. His eyes fell on Moses. Even without the huge scar and prison attire, Fulton recognized him. "Isaiah? Isaiah, help me."

Margo laughed caustically. "Help you? Honey, maybe I should explain a few things to you. No one is going to help you. You, sweetheart, are about to die, and you are going to die the way my daughter and her friend died. With sexual degradation, absolute humiliation, an immense amount of pain, and finally, if you're lucky, a relatively quick death by asphyxiation. You, Mr. Fulton, have the advantage of knowing exactly where you stand. I want you to know precisely what you have to look forward to, unlike your victims, who had no clue what you had in store for them." She stood directly in front of him.

"You're crazy! They'll catch you! You'll never get …" Fulton ranted.

"I'll never get away with it?" Margo finished his sentence for him. "Oh, honey, first they have to catch me. Then," she continued, "there's always that insanity plea. And who's crazier than the mother of a brutally murdered girl?" She leaned closer, and whispered softly in his ear, "Oh, I'll get away with it all right." Margo stood erect, and walked back across the room to her entourage. "I'd like to introduce my friends to you. I believe you've met a few of them." She stopped in front of Moses. "This is Moses, or as you know him, Isaiah. Moses was a wonderful police officer, until some little asshole about your age shot and killed his partner and blew out his kneecap. It left Moses a little bitter. I don't really think he's rooting for you," She added sarcastically. She took a few steps and stopped in front of Raul. "You may remember this clean-cut young man as your friend with the mop, Lopez." Raul nodded in Fulton's direction. "Raul lost his younger sister to a group of brutal gang members, who raped and tortured her to death. Again, I don't think he's going to be of much help to you." Standing beside Raul was Doug. His jaw was tense, his arms folded. "Doug was your getaway driver. You probably don't recognize him without the hooded jacket. He lost his elderly mother to a kid also about your age. He raped an old lady, beat her mercilessly with a bat, and left her to die on the floor of her home. Sadly, Doug never got to release the pent-up anger that murder caused. Hopefully, you can help with that." Margo held up her right hand and introduced the rest of the crew. "Then we have our FX expert, Alex. He helped greatly with your escape. Thank you, Alex. Then we have Peta, Georgia, Melanie, and Bernadette." They nodded at the mention of their names. "Every single one of them has lost someone special through the violent and deviant actions of pieces of shit like you. Do you really think you're walking out of here, Mr. Fulton?"

"So what are you going to do?" Fulton said smirking. "Fucking rape me?"

"You know, Mr. Fulton, I'm almost happy to see that defiant attitude. It makes this easier, almost enjoyable." Margo walked over to the door. "I have someone I want you to meet," she said, pulling on the handle.

The door swung open, and a middle-aged man wearing shabby clothes entered the room. The smell of sweat was suddenly apparent. The man was obese, and in the lack of air conditioning, the sweat trickled down his face. He ran the back of his chubby hand over his bald head, then wiped it on his grubby, wrinkled pants. His polo shirt was soiled with food stains down the front and heavily soaked at the armpits. He carried a large, doctor-style, black leather bag. He looked down at Simon Fulton, naked and secured to the giant ring on the floor. The man's eyes seemed to glaze over. He licked his lips.

"This," Margo said, "is Dimitri Kostopoulos. We found him via a friend of ours in records. He was actually quite easy to contact online. Apparently, Dimitri normally likes them younger, say between seven and ten, but when he saw a picture of your pretty face he made an exception to the rule. Especially when we told him that he would be your first man. That excited him. Oh, and the promise of five grand sweetened the deal. We told him that he could use all his toys, and there were no restrictions to what he could do — no time limit — and he could make as much noise as he wanted. All we asked was that you be alive when he's done."

"You can't fucking do this!" Fulton screamed. He started to pull on the rope that secured his wrists.

"We're not going to do anything, Simon," Margo cooed. "We're not even going to be in the room. We're going to be right on the other side of that mirror. Apparently, Dimitri performs better with an audience." The crew began to shuffle through the door.

"You can't do this!" Fulton screamed again. Margo looked back at him through the open door, smiling as she slowly pulled it closed behind her. He anxiously glanced over at Dimitri who had spread an array of leather and metal contraptions on the floor. He suddenly felt nauseous and was sweating. It was a cold sweat of fear. His eyes grew large with horror as he saw Dimitri once more lick his lips and slowly unzip his pants.

Chapter Forty-Six

Dimitri Kostopoulos knelt naked and exhausted before the trembling body of Simon Fulton. His large gelatinous body shook with every labored breath he drew. He ran his hand over the curve of Fulton's right buttock, sighing. Fulton quickly squirmed away from his touch in panic. He drew his knees up to his chest in as close to a fetal position as his bound hands would allow and sobbed pitifully. If only he had a little more time, Kostopoulos thought to himself, he could end this properly. Because they wouldn't let him do that, he didn't feel as though he was really finished. He wasn't completely sated. He would probably need to find another one soon to satisfy his needs. One who wasn't still moving at the end of it.

Margo entered the room. A heavy smell of sweat hung in the air. She wrinkled her nose in disgust. She had not been able to watch the whole scene of sex and debauchery the way she thought she could. Kostopoulos made her skin crawl. He had served a purpose here today, but that did not mean his actions were found to be anything other than obscene. She had had to leave the room way before Kostopoulos had taken a bolt cutter to Fulton's small toe. She found his need to take a body part as a memento especially disturbing. His final act was ordinarily ejaculation as he choked his victim to death with a piece of nylon rope. He had been denied that pleasure today. It didn't quite fit in with her agenda.

"Thank you, Mr. Kostopoulos," Margo said without emotion. "Your contribution today was greatly appreciated." Kostopoulos looked up at her through thick black eyebrows. He seemed to be totally un-phased by the fact that he was naked in front of a complete stranger. "As we promised, you will be well rewarded for your actions here today." Kostopoulos smiled greedily. He licked his lips in anticipation, and smiled again. "In fact, Mr. Kostopoulos, we're going to pay you extra for your previous endeavors." Kostopoulos raised his eyebrows, puzzled. Without warning, from behind two strong hands quickly wrapped a piece of nylon rope around Kostopoulos' neck and pulled tight. His fat fingers flew up to his throat and fought to remove the cord that was now biting into his flesh.

"You were never paid for your part in the death of eight-year-old Darren Leachman," Margo said icily. "You remember Darren, don't you, Dimitri? You took him from a playground where he waited for his mom after school. I think you still have his left ear." Margo spat the words into his now blue face. "There wasn't enough physical evidence to indict you, but the police knew it was you. You'd done it before in New Jersey, hadn't you? But there wasn't enough evidence there, either. Well, guess what? We don't need fucking evidence; you just gave us a full display. I pronounce you guilty, you fat fuck!" The strong hands pulled tighter behind Kostopoulos' neck, cutting deeper into the flesh. Blood began to trickle from the now-open skin. The hands were relentless, untiring, while Kostopoulos' own bloated hands hung limply at his sides. His dead eyes stared at the ceiling, the whites now filled with red from traumatic hemorrhaging. Doug finally released his grip on the cord, and Kostopoulos fell in a lifeless heap to the floor.

Margo turned her attention to Simon Fulton. He had wiggled himself as far away as he could, while still tethered to the floor, trying desperately to put distance between himself and the display of violence before him. His legs were stained red where he had frantically writhed around in the pool of blood from his own amputation.

"So, Mr. Fulton. Not so tough, are we?" she asked rhetorically. "Now you know you're not the only sick bastard on the face of the planet," she smiled wickedly. "So now do you think you have any of idea of how my daughter felt before she died?"

"She felt pretty good to me," Fulton answered with a forced, crooked smile.

Moses and Doug walked across the room quickly. Each took a hold of one of Fulton's ankles. They pulled his body down quickly until his hands were drawn-up tightly above his head. They yanked his legs apart violently, exposing his manhood.

"Still defiant, Mr. Fulton," Margo said, bending down to retrieve a large knife from beside Kostopoulos' bag of tricks. "Like I said before, it makes this easier."

Chapter Forty-Seven

Margo's eyes were fixated on Simon Fulton's lifeless body, while Peta, Georgia and Melanie flitted around wiping down surfaces with rags soaked in alcohol. The men were busy checking around the bodies to make sure that absolutely no incriminating evidence had been left. Moses took a plastic bag from his pocket and retrieved their trademark business card from it. He placed it on the center of Kostopoulos' forehead, he placed a second, on Fulton's chest.

"You ready to get out of here, Margo?" he asked.

"Nearly," Margo said. She began to peel back the latex gloves she had been wearing.

"No, Margo!" Peta shrieked. "Leave them on until we are outside."

"It's okay, Peta," she said comfortingly. She stuffed the gloves into one pocket, and then reached into the other. She pulled out a packet of Marlboro Lights and a Bic. Casually, she placed one of the cigarettes in her mouth and lit up. She inhaled deeply and blew out the smoke through softly-puckered lips.

"What the hell are you doing?" Moses asked, startled.

"I'm ending this the way he did," Margo said.

"What? You can't leave the cigarette. There'll be DNA on it." Moses moved toward her, Margo raised her hand.

"It's over for me, Moses," she said softly. She took another draw on the cigarette. "Audrey called me last night," she said exhaling a thin line of smoke. "Sawyer got the court order approved. He's picking up the attendance list for the group at nine o'clock. The only names from this crew that will be on it are mine and Doug's. The rest of you had completed your mandatory sessions. You weren't on the roster anymore. Nobody from this group can be linked to any of the murders. Georgia never told anyone that Moon was coming to get her granddaughter. That was a drug deal gone wrong, remember? Plus we never left a card. The Solomons never called the police, so Cicci and Venetti can't be linked to them. They already tracked

Lewis to Audrey, but she has the perfect alibi for that, and there's no evidence to link him to any of you. Dix, Delgado, and Chavez were never tied to, or prosecuted for the death of Raul's sister, so Raul won't be linked to them. His name won't show up on the list anyway. Then we have this," she said, pointing to the two bodies before her. "There's nothing to tie Doug into this, so he's safe, but like I said, my name is on the list, and everyone knows I'm linked to this piece of shit." She flicked her ash in Fulton's direction. "So I guess this is the end of the line for me. I'm going to leave a little evidence here at the scene of the crime, then I'm going home to have a bubble bath and a few hours sleep. I'll get up early and have on full makeup and a smile when Detective Sawyer arrives at my home."

"No, Margo. There has to be another way, we ..." Peta argued.

"She's right," Doug interrupted. "She's always right." He walked over to Margo with open arms. The two hugged warmly. "You have enough money to get the hell out of here," he added. "You don't have to go down for this. You can vanish."

"Where am I going to go? I mean, is there anyone in the valley who doesn't know who I am?" She smiled warmly, and wiped away a solitary tear that had run down Doug's cheek.

"There's Mexico," Peta offered.

"Mexico is for Mexicans and tourists. No thanks," she said, flicking the ash again from the cigarette.

"What about Canada?" Moses said.

"What about Canada?" Margo said, turning up her lip.

"I still know people in Brazil," Peta suggested. "They would never find you there."

"I'm not running. I did this. I'm not proud of it, but it's my crime. I need to take credit for it, and I'll gladly pay for it. Excuse me," she said, as she stepped forward. Crouching down, she stubbed out her cigarette right between Simon Fulton's eyes.

Chapter Forty-Eight

Margo looked back at the stolen furniture van that had just dropped her off. She gave a wave. Doug waved back. There was a sadness in his expression that she had never seen before. She sighed deeply and set off in the direction of her car. It had begun to rain lightly. It felt good after the stuffiness of the old police precinct. Margo climbed into the Lexus and started the engine. On the seat beside her was a zippered case she retrieved from the box Cassi had shipped home from Harvard. Inside was an assortment of CDs. She flicked through the cases without much consideration and picked one by Linkin Park, another by Three Days Grace, and a third by Green Day. At least she had heard of these. She fed them into the new CD player, and not being an aficionado of the bands, hit the random button.

She opted for the ocean highway. At this time of night there was nothing much to see, but it was still comforting to her to know she was close to the water. The ocean had been her salvation these last six months. The rain picked up a little. She turned on the windshield wipers, and put on a faster setting. The tempo of the blades on the glass complemented Linkin Park's, "What I've Done" which had just begun, like a form of percussion, drawing Margo's attention to it. She'd heard the song many times before on the radio. It was one of Cassi's favorites. Only now, the lyrics seemed to wrap themselves around her brain.…

So let mercy come … And wash away … What I've done

The lyrics seemed to lodge themselves forcefully inside Margo's head. It was as if the singer knew what she had done and was scolding her, chastising her. Tears flowed easily and heavily down her cheeks. She was not sure exactly what the tears were for. Did they represent remorse for the monster she had become? Were they the suppressed anger she felt for a society that had failed her and her daughter? Or perhaps they were the result of the agony that churned inside her, every waking moment, eating away at her heart, mind, and soul. The same agony that had been the only reason for her existence. It had motivated her to get up every day. It had directed her every thought and action. It had pushed her to do things, that six months ago, would have been totally abhorrent to her nature. Things that she could never atone for, never forget, and yet, would never regret. The agony had served a purpose, and now its purpose was gone.

The sound of tires on gravel let Margo know she was home. Automatically, she put the car in park and removed the keys from the ignition. It had stopped raining. She walked up the front steps to the house, suddenly realizing that she hadn't put the car in the garage and that she remembered absolutely nothing of the drive home. Her mind was on auto-pilot. She shrugged and turned the key in the lock. Inside was a familiar, pleasant odor of vanilla and spice, mixed with the natural aroma of the ocean. It told her she was home, but it didn't feel like home, not anymore. The soft padding of Annie's paws on the tile greeted her. Gently she patted the dog's head. Annie sniffed at her clothes, and then, as though she had smelled something repugnant quickly ran off. Margo placed her keys on the hall table and casually dropped her purse to the ground. Kicking off her shoes, she walked toward the back of the house. The marble felt cool on her feet. She unbuttoned the cuffs of her silk blouse, and then proceeded to unfasten the rest. It was damp from the rain, causing the natural fabric to give off its own odious perfume. It was the smell of rain and raw silk, with a side of blood and death thrown in. She removed the shirt and threw it to the floor. She unzipped her skirt and let it fall, casually stepping out of it. Reaching up, she removed the jeweled barrette which secured her mane of red hair. She shook her head from side to side, letting the hair cascade around her face, as she threw the barrette onto the nearest sofa. She paused in the kitchen long enough to remove her expensive, designer watch and rings, which she nonchalantly dropped into an empty fruit bowl, and then continued out onto the patio. The air was cool and fresh out here. It smelled of shells, seaweed, and salt. Margo smiled. Now she was home. Deftly, in the dark, she made her way down the stone steps to the sandy cove below. She could do this with her eyes closed. The dark did not slow her down one bit. The cool sand felt good on her feet. She curled and relaxed her toes, gripping the damp grains.

The water splashing over her feet told Margo that it was high tide. In the dark, Margo couldn't really tell how high it was, but she knew it wouldn't get much higher. The water only ever came halfway into the cove. It would go out soon, taking with it whatever was in the cove. She stepped deeper into the brine, shivering. The moonlight illuminated the opening to the beach. She headed for it now, wading waist deep through the water. Annie's nervous barking echoed from the stone steps behind her. She would not venture into the cove at night, especially at high tide; smart dog.

"It's okay, baby," Margo called back soothingly. Annie seemed to be adequately comforted, her barking stopped. "Everything's okay now," she said, as she dove headfirst into the cool black water.

Chapter Forty-Nine

Rick Sawyer entered the investigation room holding two foam cups. He held one out in Jim's direction.

"Cream, no sugar," he said.

"Thanks." Jim eagerly accepted the coffee. "So when do I get to see my wife?"

"Your wife?" Sawyer asked. "I thought you were divorced."

"My ex-wife," Jim corrected himself.

"I'll take you over there shortly," Sawyer told him. "There are just a few loose ends I need to tie up. I'd like to ask you a few questions if I may."

"Do I need an attorney?" Jim asked.

"Not yet," Sawyer answered with a smile. He opened a large manila envelope and pulled out two large black-and-white photographs from a pack of a dozen or so. He threw them on the desk in front of Jim. They were the crime scene photos of a Hispanic-looking male lying on a sidewalk covered in blood. His body lay in a mangled heap.

"Ever see this guy before?" Sawyer asked.

"That's a guy?" Jim answered in a shocked voice. "What the hell happened to him? He's a mess!"

"We think your ex-wife's car happened to him. A pawn shop security camera caught her plate leaving the scene. Ever see him with her?" Sawyer lifted the photo closer to Jim's face.

"God, no!" Jim replied. "My wife never hung out with people like that!" Even through the blood and carnage, Jim could tell this was street trash.

"Can you identify this vehicle?" Sawyer asked, dropping a rather grainy surveillance picture of a man getting out of a black car. It appeared to have been taken in a parking garage.

"Sure. That's Margo's car," Jim verified. He recognized the man in the picture as himself. "I used it to drive myself to LAX a few days after Margo got out of the hospital."

"Yep," Sawyer said nodding. "That puts you in the car two days after it was reportedly destroyed in a garage fire."

"There was a fire?" Jim asked innocently.

"Reportedly," Sawyer answered.

"What about this guy?" Sawyer said, adding another couple of pictures. They were of Lewis' bloody remains on a sidewalk.

"I've never seen him before in my life. Who the hell is he?" Jim leaned forward in his chair to inspect the image.

"How about these?" Sawyer dropped three more pictures onto the table. There was one of a man with a large gunshot wound to the chest, and two more of the mangled remains of what looked like men lying in the desert. "These were members of a motorcycle gang. Ring a bell?"

"Ring a bell? I'm a movie director! Why the hell would these ring a bell?" Jim put his hands up in the air.

"Okay," Sawyer said without emotion. "Try these." He dropped a photo of a dead gunman on a liquor shop floor, followed by a picture of a naked fat man with nylon rope around his neck. "Notice any similarities?"

"What's that card thing on his forehead?" Jim asked.

"Oh. You noticed that?" Sawyer goaded him. "Ever see it before?" He pointed to a card laying on the gunman's chest, and another one on the biker with the gunshot. He picked up the picture of Lewis. "This guy had one in his pocket," he added coolly.

"What is it? A business card?"

"I guess so, if you're in the business of murder." Sawyer pulled a plastic bag from his pocket which held a card inside. "Seen these cards before?"

"You think I did this?" Jim asked astounded.

"No, Mr. Marsden," Sawyer said calmly. "We know who did this." He placed one more photograph on the table. "Recognize this one?"

"Oh, my God!" he whispered in disbelief. He picked up the photograph of Simon Fulton and stared at the grotesque scene. "What the fuck happened to him. Why the hell is he that color?"

"He was asphyxiated," Sawyer told him. "Someone stuffed his own dick down his throat."

Jesus, Margo! Jim thought to himself. *What the hell did you do?*

Chapter Fifty

Margo stared down at her French manicure. Shit, she thought, these were going to look terrible growing out. It was a shame the California penal system would not allow Lynn, her nail tech, in for a visit. Maybe she could request a manicure once a month, in lieu of conjugal visits. She smiled at the thought.

"So, I take it you still have no intention of cooperating, Ms. Priestley," Sawyer's voice droned through her imagination.

"Oh! I'm sorry. Are you still here?" Margo replied sarcastically.

"Break a nail?" Sawyer asked.

"No, you did, when you dragged me into that goddamn boat." Margo shot him a dirty look. "I wonder if that falls under police brutality."

"What do you think what you did to Simon Fulton falls under?" Sawyer rested his face in his palm.

"A necessary evil," she retorted. "I told you, I don't regret what I did."

"A necessary evil?" Sawyer shook his head. "You mutilated the fucking kid!"

"Detective Sawyer," Margo stared at him defiantly. "The fucking kid made my daughter beg for her life. I made him beg for his death. I think that's fair."

"Absolutely no remorse; huh, Margo?"

"Absolutely none," she answered coolly.

"Is that why you tried to kill yourself?" Sawyer asked flatly. "Again?"

"I was trying to avoid this ridiculous bantering, Detective Sawyer." Margo placed a strand of loose hair behind her ear, and then rested her chin on her hand, mimicking Sawyer. "I already admitted everything. Just lock me up."

"Just as soon as you tell me who was helping you," Sawyer smiled. "You can't tell me Fulton just lay there and let you go Bobbitt on him."

"I acted completely alone," Margo smiled back. "I'm a very persuasive woman."

"I'm pretty persuasive myself," Sawyer said smoothly. "Look at how I persuaded that judge to grant me a subpoena twelve hours earlier. That's why I was waiting for you in the boat."

"You were only waiting in the boat, because you couldn't get a search warrant for my house in time." Margo folded her arms and leaned back in her seat. "If I hadn't gone for a swim, you'd be screwed."

"I guess I'm lucky you didn't use a razor blade again, huh?" Sawyer folded his arms, and leaned back in his chair, mimicking Margo. "So if you don't regret killing Fulton, why try to drown yourself? Why the remorse? Do you regret killing the others?"

"Which others?" Margo shrugged casually.

"The others with whom you left a card." He casually picked up his envelope of photographs which had been strategically propped up against the table leg beside him. He opened the envelope and slid a photograph across the table in front of Margo. He started with the picture of Simon Fulton. Margo looked down at the image, while Sawyer waited for a reaction. He waited in vain.

He slid the picture of Kostopoulos beside the first one. "So, how do you know this guy?" he asked. Margo was steadfast in her resolve to be inanimate. "Do you have any recollection of this one?" he persisted, throwing the pictures, one on top of the others. "No? How about these?" He continued pitching the photos as deftly as a Las Vegas double-deck dealer. "Nothing to say? No reasons to offer me on why you killed these guys? Okay, I'll give you another chance," he said, pitching yet another picture onto the pile. "Now I know you know this guy." Margo stared at the picture out of the corner of her eye. She frowned at the image of Jim getting out of her BMW, not quite sure when it was taken.

"You're following Jim around?" she questioned.

"Not Jim," Sawyer answered. "This picture was taken a few days after you were released from the hospital. But more importantly," he continued, "two days after the car he was driving was supposedly destroyed in a fire. A fire, which incidentally, he doesn't recall." Margo did not look up. "Then we have this guy," Sawyer said, slapping yet another photo on the table. "Do you know this guy, Margo? This one didn't have a card on him." Again Margo stared out of the corner of her eye at the photo of the Hispanic man she had almost cut in half with her BMW. She raised her hands and began to massage her temples with her fingertips.

"I don't know who he is," she answered innocently.

"His name *was* Hector Sanchez," Sawyer informed her. "He was a known drug dealer and pimp — liked to get rough with his ladies. Apparently he was getting rough with one of his girls when some lady in a black sedan crushed him against a wall. The girl remembered two white women in the car. Who was with you, Margo?" Sawyer leaned into the table.

"I don't know what you're talking about. I've never seen this guy before in my life," Margo said, leaning forward to match Sawyer's glare.

"Okay, have it your way," Sawyer said. He slapped a pile of papers hard on the table in front of her. "Want to explain some of these bank withdrawals?"

"Not really, no," Margo sighed.

"Okay then," Sawyer continued. "June twenty-eighth, ten thousand dollars withdrawn; July sixth, fifteen thousand dollars withdrawn; July twentieth, two days before we found Cicci and Venetto, you took out another fifteen thousand dollars. Here, three days before Fulton escaped from prison, you took five hundred thousand out of an account. What was it, Margo? Look the other way money? Who did you pay?"

"I went to Vegas," she sighed heavily. "Any law against that?"

"Any one who can verify that?" Sawyer asked without expression.

"I can't remember the dealer's name; I think it was Shirley."

"Which hotel was it?"

"I think it was the Encore. No, Bellagio. Could have been the MGM. I was a little drunk," she raised her palms in innocence.

"And nobody saw Margo Priestley staggering around Vegas shit-faced?" Sawyer rolled his eyes.

"I had on sweats and a ball cap," Margo offered in her defense. "No one dresses in Vegas anymore."

"Who did you go with?" Sawyer shook his head.

"I'm sorry, I can't tell you." She put her index finger up to her lips. "Shh; What happens in Vegas, stays in Vegas." She winked at Sawyer.

"Okay, Margo, have it your way." He pulled one final picture from the envelope. "It seems the pawn shop security camera across the street caught the license plate of a black car leaving the murder scene. Recognize the plate number?" He threw one last grainy picture across the table. The picture could have been of any dark car in the night, except for the fact that the car passed under a street light, completely illuminating the rear plate. "This picture was taken months after your supposed garage fire."

"How do you know someone didn't steal my plates?" Margo retorted defiantly.

"I don't, and that is a very real possibility. However, there is still this photo here of your ex-husband in your supposedly destroyed BMW, taken two days after the alleged fire." Margo sat quietly. Sawyer smiled. "I had a nice chat with Carla, your housekeeper. Funny, she didn't recall a fire, either."

"She doesn't know much about anything," she said smiling. "I think she drinks."

Sawyer shook his head. "So here's the thing, Margo. I checked over the paperwork for your auto claim, and as coincidence would have it, it appears that the fire marshal that inspected your garage is actually in the very same support group as you."

"He had nothing to do with it!" Margo snapped. "I asked him to sign off on some papers for me. He didn't know anything about it. He was a little star-struck. I took advantage of him," she said coolly, trying to regain her composure. She knew she wasn't very convincing.

"Well, that might be true, but you know what? I have a feeling that if I subpoena all the attendance records of the group for the last year, I might just be able to tie somebody into something. But for right now, I'm just going to hold your buddy, Doug." Sawyer rose from the table and turned toward the door.

"For what? Falsifying documents?" she gasped. "He could lose his job for that!"

"Try accessory to murder!" Sawyer snapped as he turned to face her. "He's going to lose a lot more than his job."

Margo swallowed hard. This was not how it was supposed to work out. Damn the car, damn the security camera, and damn the airport surveillance. Damn!

"So I'll ask you one more time," Sawyer smiled smugly. "Who was in the car with you?"

Chapter Fifty-One

Doug rubbed his eyes, but stopped when his fingers inadvertently touched the tender bruise on his left cheekbone. He winced, and allowed his finger to trace a path to the open cut across the bridge of his nose. *Shit, that's gonna leave a scar*, he thought vainly. He gently measured the play in his nose, with his thumb and forefinger. It hurt like hell, but it didn't feel broken, well not like the other times anyway. He sniffed loudly and wiped the end of his nose on the back of his hand. He examined his hand casually. At least the damn thing had stopped bleeding. He looked up as the door across the interrogation room opened and Sawyer and Sanchez entered.

"Fucking Keystone Kops are here!" He said sarcastically.

"We prefer Laurel and Hardy." Sawyer admonished him.

"So which one are you?"

Sawyer opened his jacket and looked down at his distinct lack of abdominal flab. "I think it's obvious I'm Laurel." He stated.

"Thanks a fucking lot!" Sanchez called from across the room, straddling a chair backwards.

"How's the nose?" Sawyer asked.

"How's the lip?" Doug sneered.

Sawyer traced the outer corner of his mouth with the tip of his tongue. "Not bad. I've had worse." He stared at the nasty gash. "You need more ice?"

"You should give it to him." Doug nodded in Sanchez' direction. "He looks like he could use it." Sanchez glared back at Doug with his one good eye. His left was almost closed shut, and was already blacking up. His bottom lip looked like it belonged to a Mursi tribes-woman. "Try fucking knocking next time!" Doug advised loudly.

"Try not resisting fucking arrest next time!" Sanchez spat.

"Arrest? That's how you fucking arrest someone? Getting 'em in a choke hold?" Doug smiled a crooked, wicked kind of smile. The memory of the way he had flipped Sanchez, and then delivered two well-aimed, powerful rights, still delighted him. "Good job pretty boy here, was there to save your ass." He taunted.

"Fuck you." Sanchez had no better comeback.

"So Ryan, still no idea why you're here?" Sawyer queried.

"Unpaid parking ticket?" Doug offered.

"No, but funnily enough it does come down to paperwork," Sawyer said smiling. He gently placed a stack of photographs in front of Doug, and then fanned them smoothly, in a large arc. They were all the victims of the Support Group.

"Who are these?" Doug asked innocently. "The last people you arrested?"

"That's a good one." Sawyer chuckled. "I like that. Actually, I was hoping you could tell me why these people died the way they did. The reasoning behind the various modus operandi."

"How would I know?" Doug shrugged casually.

"Well I'm not sure yet, but I think they might all be connected to a certain counseling group, that you're a member of."

"That *I'm* a member of?" Doug shook his head. He leaned forward to inspect the photographs again. "These people weren't in any group I'm in."

"Come on Ryan. Take a good look." Sawyer leaned down to look Doug in the eyes. "I already have you on resisting arrest, and assault on a police officer. Don't make me add more charges."

"Like what?" Doug asked defiantly.

"Well," Sawyer placed the photo of Jim alighting from Margo's car on the table. "There's fraud for a start." He placed a pink carbon copy of the Fire Marshall's report for Margo's car at the side of the photo. He pointed to the digital time and date displayed on the bottom right corner of the surveillance photograph. "These dates don't quite tally up Doug. It would appear that Mr. Marsden was out and about in a car that was already burnt to a crisp, according to you."

"I must have got the dates wrong." Doug said with a small sigh.

"I guess you must have." Sawyer dropped another picture onto the table. "Then we have this. This kinda looks like falsifying documents to conceal a crime to me." He pointed to the illuminated shot of Margo's rear license plate. "That's tampering with evidence. Makes you an accessory after the fact."

"Okay, you got me." Doug held up his hands. "I was a little smitten. I signed off on some papers for a beautiful woman. She told me she had been in an accident. I wanted to help her out. Is that so bad?"

"I call that commendable." Sawyer nodded his head in approval. "However, the courts could call it accessory to murder." He placed the picture, of the almost cut in half pimp, on top of the pile.

"Shit!" Doug said, blowing out. "I never thought of it like that. Maybe I should get a lawyer."

"Maybe you should." Sawyer said calmly. "Like the Miranda rights state, as I told you earlier, if you can not afford…"

"I don't believe that's going to be a problem here," Jack Ross' voice said sternly. "Mr. Ryan is now my client."

"Ross?" Sawyer looked puzzled. "You're State Prosecutor! How…"

"Not any longer Detective Sawyer. I'm now in private practice, and Mr. Ryan here has retained my services." Ross took a seat across from Doug, and began opening the attaché case he had placed on the table before him. He looked up at Sawyer with raised eyebrows. "Thank you, I'd like some time alone with my client, if you don't mind. This interrogation is over."

Chapter Fifty-Two

Margo noticed, on examination, what appeared to be dried saliva spots covering the talking end of the telephone handset. Her stomach lurched in disgust. What she wouldn't give for a wet wipe right now.

"Margo!" Jim's voice sounded agitated. "Would you put the phone up to your ear, please. I'm trying to talk to you." She reluctantly complied. "I don't know what I'm supposed to say to these guys. You haven't told me anything!"

"So that's exactly what you tell them," Margo answered calmly.

"They're asking all kinds of questions about your car, and a fire, and some drug dealer you hit! What's going on?" He spat the words into the handset in a forced whisper.

"Jim, don't worry. You don't know anything that can get me in trouble. Just tell them the truth. Just tell them what you know," she smiled weakly.

"That's just it! I don't know anything! You haven't told me a goddamn thing! What the hell's going on?" He leaned towards the plexiglass that separated them. "Did you do that to Fulton? Did you kill him?"

"Yes," she said. "Yes, I did." She placed her hand on the plastic that separated them. "I did it for Cassi." Jim placed his hand on the other side, in a show of solidarity.

"Hands down from the glass!" the guard stationed by the door ordered. Like children reprimanded in a classroom, they both obeyed immediately.

"I'll be there tomorrow," Jim informed her.

"You don't need to be there," Margo said sullenly. "It's just a formality, really. I've pled guilty to everything, so there won't be a trial. I guess I still have to be formally charged with the murders, and then, at some point they'll sentence me. The press will be all over it. You might want to stay away."

"I'll be there tomorrow," Jim reinforced.

"Jim, please don't …" she began, but faltered.

"Don't what?"

"Don't … Please don't bring Brigitte." She pleaded with her eyes. "This has nothing to do with …

"She's in Paris," he interrupted. "She got a talk show deal."

"Oh!" She picked at a loose thread on her prison-issue dress. "So you're moving over there?"

"No; just Brigitte," Jim shrugged. "She left a couple of weeks ago. They start recording at the end of this month."

"So it's permanent?" Margo was trying hard not to smile. She didn't know why she felt so happy. It wasn't as though they could rekindle their relationship now.

"Well, she got a two-year contract. I guess it's pretty permanent."

"So how come you didn't go with her?" Margo tried to sound casual.

"She said I was spending too much time with you. She thinks I'm still in love with you," Jim exhaled loudly. "She's right."

"Oh!" For the first time in a long while, she was speechless.

"So I guess I'd better get used to phone sex." He raised his eyebrows playfully.

"Five minutes," the guard warned.

"Jim. I don't want you to waste your time here," she said softly.

"Shut up, Margo," Jim answered firmly.

"Jim, I'm serious. I'm never getting out of here."

"You don't know that."

"Oh, I know it," she smiled. "You're the only one who doesn't know it yet. But you have to accept it, Jim."

"Shut up, Margo." He sighed heavily. "I'm having dinner with Jack tonight. He's going to let me know what our options are."

"Jack Ross?" she asked, surprised. "He's a state prosecutor. Can he give advice on my case?"

"I don't see why not! He's not on your case. He was supposed to be prosecuting Fulton, remember? Well, until you did what you did." He shrugged. "Anyway, he called me. We're just going to have something casual. Someplace the paparazzi won't be."

"Give him my love," Margo added softly.

"Do it yourself, when you get out of here," he ordered defiantly.

"Okay, Jim! Keep the faith, babe," she said sarcastically.

"Will do." Jim looked up at the approaching guard. "Looks like you have to go." He stared back at Margo, his eyes sorrowful. "I love you, Margo," he said as the guard tapped Margo on the shoulder, indicating the visit was over.

"I love you, too," she answered sweetly, replacing the handset, without looking at him. She stood and turned quickly, managing not to make eye contact. She padded softly ahead of the guard through a heavy metal door, wiping her cheek with the back of her hand.

Chapter Fifty-Three

The drive from the Linwood Women's Jail to the Beverly Hills Courthouse normally took thirty to forty minutes, depending on traffic. Margo would have that time alone to compose herself and get ready for the throngs of photographers and fans who would no doubt be in attendance, waiting to catch a shot of her through the prison bus window. She had caught a few moments of the local news last night, which had declared her to be a suspect in the alleged abduction and murder of Simon Fulton, and in the last few days even the national broadcasts had speculated on her involvement in this heinous crime. Her scheduled court appearance had been well-publicized. There should be a good turnout, she thought.

It felt good to be out of prison garb. Jim had brought her pale green Prada linen suit, black lace camisole, and low black pumps. She wore her hair in a low bun at the nape of her neck. Even without makeup, she looked fresh and elegant in her own clothes. She could have been attending a luncheon date, job interview, or a business meeting in her present attire, but instead, would today have charges leveled against her. The only flaw in her appearance today was the poor choice in jewelry bestowed upon her by the California Department of Corrections. The shackles did no justice at all to her Jimmy Choos, and made her usually graceful gait somewhat awkward. Her hands were manacled, with a chain running from the cuffs to the shackles, reminiscent of a chain-gang prisoner. She could not imagine walking miles along the edge of a road in these, even without the Choos. Thank God, they would soon be removed at the courthouse.

"How come I'm the only one on the bus?" Margo wondered aloud.

"Well, firstly, yours is a high profile case," the defense attorney informed her, "and secondly, not too many cases are heard in Beverley Hills. It appears you're the only game in town today." She pulled a large yellow legal pad out of her shabby briefcase, and began to make notes.

"These seats need more padding," Margo said to the armed guard sitting in the corner, his back to the security screen which separated the driver from the occupants of the bus. "I'm getting bruised."

"Leave him alone, Margo," Catherine Siegel teased. "He's only a baby." She went back to perusing the legal pad she now had on her lap. This was a great case for her, if only Margo would let her in, she thought. Jim had hired the best in the business, an attorney named Stewart Moore, highly recommended by Jack Ross, but Margo had refused all legal counsel, especially from Siegel. In fact, Margo had told her to get the hell out more than once. Finally, Catherine explained that she would stay on the sidelines in case, at any time, Margo decided she needed her. It was only on Moore's insistence that Siegel was actually on the bus at all. He had instructed his latest hire to stay with Margo whether she liked it or not.

"I'm pleading guilty to all charges, you moron!" Margo had told her repeatedly. "There is no case here! I don't need you!"

"Well, I need to be there to tell the judge that you have declined counsel and defense," Catherine had argued, getting on the bus. "And I was told that I had to ride the bus with you." She went back to making notes.

"Whatever," Margo conceded. Catherine had a real get-on-your-nerves way about her.

"Where are we?" Catherine said, looking up from her pad.

Margo had been resting her eyes, trying to ignore Catherine. She opened one eye and peered out the wire grid-clad window. "Looks like the hills up past Santa Monica," she said with little interest.

"There's a bad accident on I-405," the guard said in a deep masculine voice. "We have to take a detour."

"Oh, okay," Catherine muttered and went back to her legal pad.

Margo had driven to Beverley Hills many times. She was familiar with the surrounding areas, but she did not recognize where they were now. "What road are we on?" she asked. The guard shrugged. The bus seemed to be climbing away from the city. Clouds of dust flew up around the windows, which told Margo this was not a paved highway. They were on an inner road, with rocks on either side of them. This was definitely not the scenic route. Up ahead was road construction, at a fork in the dirt road. The left lane had a 'road closed' sign in front of it, and so traffic was being detoured to the right. Margo looked at the small crew of workers. "What are they doing all the way out here?" she asked as the bus took the road to the right.

"Maybe there was a rockslide," Catherine answered disinterested.

"What road are we on?" Margo asked again. She tried to see over her shoulder through the dirty bus windows. There were no street signs here, or directional billboards. They were up in the hills, with only rocks, dirt, and dust. Margo tried to stand up to get a better look.

"Sit down!" the guard ordered.

Margo slid back into her seat. She shrugged her shoulders and raised her eyebrows. Hey, it was no skin off her nose if they got lost. It wasn't as though they could give her extra time for being late. She focused on the road ahead, oblivious to the goings-on behind her. She might have been a little more concerned, had she seen the road workers behind her, pick up the 'road closed' sign and place it in front of the right lane, immediately after the bus passed through.

Chapter Fifty-Four

The bus ride had certainly become bumpier since the detour, and they were definitely traveling at an incline. Something about this felt wrong, smelled wrong. The bus windows had not been cleaned in some time, obscuring Margo's view. A strange droning sound came from outside, like a distant engine, or an overhead jet. It appeared to be getting closer. The guard sat up straight in his seat, as if suddenly aware of apparent danger.

"What is it?" Catherine asked in her nasal tone. The guard ignored her, apparently trying to get a better look through the window. He leaned closer to the glass. As he did, the window suddenly shattered, and at the same time the side of his head exploded. He fell forward, slumped through the now-open window. The bus lurched wildly to the left as the driver reacted to the sudden attack.

"Get down!" he yelled back at the two women.

Catherine Siegel's screams were piercing. Her absolute hysteria was evident. If Margo's hands were free she would have slapped her hard, but seeing as she was shackled she would have to endure the high-pitch cries escaping the frantic attorney. The engine sounds grew louder and through the blown-out window Margo could see the outlines of men on motorcycles through the dust. They were all around the bus, trying to force it off the road. The bus followed the curve in the road to the right. Through the clouds of dust, Margo could see what looked like a group of men holding shotguns. The driver pulled hard to the left to avoid the group.

"Get down!" he screamed again loudly as the bus veered uncontrollably toward a large tree.

Both women threw themselves down onto their seats at almost the exact moment the bus hit the tree. Margo was thrown forward and ended up on the floor between her seat and the one in front. Catherine rolled on top of Margo, jamming both of them tightly in place. Catherine's screams were deafening and unending.

"Shut up!" Margo shouted, suddenly aware that the bus had stopped. "Get off me!" Catherine seemed oblivious to the fact that she was crushing Margo, and equally unaware of the heinous sounds that she was emitting.

"Shut up!" Margo growled, scrambling backward from underneath Catherine. Her rear retreat was suddenly blocked by a large pair of black boots.

"Shut the fuck up!" A deep voice ordered, as he racked a shotgun and held it to Catherine's head. The screaming stopped, replaced by a pathetic whimpering. The black boots took a step back. "Now get up!" the voice ordered. The black boots stepped back, allowing the women room to maneuver. Margo had difficulty getting to her feet with the shackles and manacles, so the shotgun wielding owner of the black boots helped her, pulling her up by the collar of her jacket. He gestured with a nod of the head to the front of the bus, where the window had been shot out. The women shuffled slowly forward, past the dead guard, their feet keeping time to Catherine's constant sobbing.

A second man, wearing a red bandana, climbed into the bus through the now open front door. "Move over!" he yelled. The terrified women moved to the two nearest seats as he raised a shotgun to the lock section of the security screen at the front of the bus. The sound was deafening as he fired the gun, disintegrating the lock. He kicked the door of the screen open. The driver began to stir in his seat, moaning loudly. The man in the red bandana took a handgun from inside his waistband, and leveled it at the man's head. As he discharged the gun, the driver's side window suddenly dripped red. Again came the frantic screaming from Catherine. "Move it!" he screamed, gesturing with the handgun for them to get off the bus. He stepped between the now dead driver and the women as they walked to the front of the bus.

Once on the ground Margo felt more confident. If these men just wanted them dead they would have just shot them like the others on the bus. Unless, of course, someone else wanted them dead. Maybe these guys were just the gophers, just here to collect. But who the hell else could it be? It was hard to concentrate with Catherine screaming like that.

"Someone shut her up!" the man in the red bandana screamed.

There was a loud thud behind her, and then Margo heard the sound of Catherine's body hitting the ground. She spun around in time to see the man with the black boots still holding the butt of his gun over Catherine's lifeless body.

"What the fuck did you do?" the man in the red bandana yelled.

"You said shut her up!" the man in the boots yelled back in his defense.

"Not fucking permanently, you idiot! She's the witness!" he stepped forward. "Is she breathing?"

A third man stepped forward and knelt down beside the unconscious woman. He held his fingertips to the side of her throat. "We have a pulse," he said quietly. He moved his hand around the back of her skull and pulled it back, now a deep red. "Nice fucking going, Rambo!" He looked up at the man in black boots. "I'm gonna give her the shot anyway. We just have to hope for the best." He pulled a small plastic case from inside his jacket, opened it, and took a small hypodermic needle. He applied enough pressure to cause a small amount of the clear liquid inside the needle to squirt out the tip, and then with a quick movement he inserted it into the top of Catherine's thigh, squeezing the rest of the contents into her body.

"What the hell is that?" Margo yelled. "What did you do to her?" The men ignored her.

"So is she gonna be okay?" the man in black boots asked.

"She'd better be, asshole," the man in the red bandana snapped. "Or you're gonna have to answer to Ross."

"Ross who?" Margo's head was whirling. She looked from one to the other. "Who the hell are you guys?"

"I'm afraid they work for me, Margo." She spun around to see the image of Jack Ross emerging from the back of a black limousine.

Chapter Fifty-Five

"Jack? What the hell are you doing?" Margo stared in disbelief at her long-time friend.

"I might have asked you the same thing," Ross answered calmly. "Sorry, Margo, but I couldn't let you go to court today. This thing has got to end." He walked toward her. "Did you know that since your little brigade began this crusade, violent crime in L.A. has dropped by seventeen percent? Seventeen percent!" he exclaimed. "When that comes out, everyone will hail you as a hero. Who the hell would want to prosecute that case? Who the hell would want to pronounce you guilty? It makes a mockery of the legal system. As flawed as it is, I can't let that happen, Margo."

"I don't understand, Jack." She looked around nervously. "Who are these guys? What the hell did you inject her with? And what was he talking about, a witness?"

"Whoa, Margo! One at a time, please!" He walked over to where Catherine lay and gently nudged her with his foot. "Miss Siegel here was supposed to be a witness to your brutal death at the hands of a biker gang, but someone put her out too soon." He did not look happy. "That's okay; we don't need anyone to witness your demise. There'll be enough physical evidence."

"You prick!" Margo shouted. "I hope they get you, you bastard!" She spat at Ross, just missing his face.

"Jesus, Margo! What the hell are you doing?" He examined his expensive suit sleeve for bodily fluids.

"If you wanted me dead, you son of a bitch, why not just kill *me*?" She looked at the body of the guard, still hanging precariously from the bus window. "You asshole! Just fucking shoot me and get it over with!"

"What?" Ross looked baffled. He turned and strode quickly in the direction of the guard. "Get up, idiot!" he shouted. Like a scene from a Michael Jackson video, the guard immediately sat upright.

"You, too, moron!" Ross yelled. The bus driver sat up and looked sheepishly around the seat.

"They told us to play dead until we were told not to," the guard said in his defense."

"Okay then, NOT TO!" Ross yelled. "Now get the hell off the bus!" The two men quickly jumped up and exited the bus. They ran in the direction of an old white transit van.

"Oh, my God!" Margo whispered. "How did you do that?" The beginnings of a smile began to touch her lips.

"Exactly how long have you been in Hollywood?" a familiar voice asked. The rear doors of the transit were now open and out climbed Alex. In his hand was a remote control with three or four toggle switches on it. He touched one of them. "This one set off the window and the guard's head." He wiggled another. "This one detonated the side of the driver's brain and the handgun. And this one," he smiled playfully, "was going to set off the rifle that shot you, and hit you with a tranq. That way you really went down. Clever, huh?" He moved toward her with his arms open. Margo tried to reciprocate, but her shackles forbade it. "Oh, for God's sake!" Alex yelled. "Someone get those awful things off her!"

"Oh, I forgot," Ross said, digging in his jacket pocket. He pulled out a small set of keys and threw them to the man in the red bandana. "Solomon, do the honors!"

"Solomon? So we finally get to meet," Margo said, as Rick Solomon unlocked her shackles. "Thank you."

"Thank you," Solomon countered. "It's nice to have something decent to fight for, and from what I've been told, I'm indebted to you."

"Okay, guys, get that thing out of here," Alex yelled. One of the biker gang jumped up in the driver's seat of the bus and started it up. Slowly the bus pulled away from the scene. In the distance, the sound of another engine could be heard. Margo looked to see a second bus approaching. Alex noticed her puzzled look. "We have a couple of John Doe volunteers, and a Jane Doe of course, to play the parts of yourself and the guards. We're going to have to actually shoot up the bus a little and set the scene with the bodies, to give our friends in forensics something to work with."

"Our friends in forensics?" Margo questioned.

"You have no idea how big this thing is, Margo," Ross interrupted, excitedly. "We have people in forensics, the medical field, law enforcement, public records, the prison system. We can falsify any document we need. We can create people at will, people with a past. We can make their school records, job history, prison record. Hell, we just killed two long-time state employees who never really existed. We could get a pension or disability if we wanted. We even have a couple of judges, but you didn't hear that from me."

"We're going to need more pins," Alex said with an excited laugh.

"I can't believe you did this," Margo shook her head, still amazed.

"You helped immensely. Well, your bank account did." Ross smiled. "Money moves mountains, and you've got enough to shift Everest. This little production hardly put a dent in it."

"How did you get to it without me?"

"Ppphhh!" Ross scoffed. "Gordie Horowitz is the greatest money launderer on the face of the planet. He's also the CFO of your bank. I got him off on embezzlement charges eight years ago. He owed me big."

"But how … how did you throw this together since last night?"

"Last night?" Ross looked puzzled. "We've been planning this since you were apprehended."

"Didn't you meet with Jim last night? I thought he said you were meeting."

"Well, yes, but this wasn't Jim's idea," Ross informed her, puffing his chest out. "I met with him to offer him a role in all this, which I might add, he accepted eagerly. He's sitting in a bodega somewhere in Mexico right now. You're going to drive across the border in the limo, and meet up with him in a few hours. He'll fly you further south to Brazil."

"But how did you get involved in all this?"

"Let's say we have a few mutual acquaintances." He smiled across at Alex.

"I called Jack as soon as they picked you up. I knew he loved you as much as I did, so I was sure he'd help. We've been good friends for a very long time."

"Ohhhhhh!" Margo exhaled slowly. She looked from Jack to Alex and back again.

"What the hell are you smiling at?" Ross asked playfully.

"Well, first, I'm so sorry I called you a prick," Margo said sheepishly. "But more than that, I'm sorry for all the women I've tried to fix you up with over the years."

"She needs to get out of here!" Solomon yelled. "We're ready to start shooting this thing up."

Margo stared open-mouthed as two men positioned a cadaver dressed as a prison guard against the bus window. Two more men carried the naked body of a woman out of the bus, and laid her strategically in the road. She was about the same size as Margo, with similar hair color, only, three quarters of her face was missing. Margo could not hide the horror she felt inside.

"She's perfect for our needs," Alex said softly. "She died horribly in the street, with no name, family, or friends. At least this way her death means something. That and she'll have the most expensive funeral in town."

"We need the clothes," Solomon yelled, "before this crazy bitch wakes up!"

Alex handed Margo a plastic bag. Inside were a full set of clothes and a blonde wig. "You can change in the van. Quick, Margo!"

Quick changes were her forte, and Margo emerged from the transit in just a couple of minutes, blonde wig slightly askew. She handed her clothes to Alex. The biker crew was having way too much fun shooting up the bus, and Ross and Solomon were yelling directives fiercely at them.

"Get in the car, Margo," Ross said firmly, walking toward her. "You have to go."

"Wait a minute," she hesitated. "What about Doug?"

"He walked a few hours ago," Ross said. "Apparently all evidence linking him to this case was lost in a computer meltdown downtown. They're still trying to figure out what happened. Sawyer handed in some paperwork before he flew out last night, but no one seems to know where it is." He raised his eyebrows playfully.

"What about when he gets back?" Margo asked concerned.

"He's not coming back!" Alex said with a giggle. "His transfer came through. He had to agree to leave for New York immediately or the position would have been offered to someone else."

"But what about his sidekick? What's his name?" Margo looked up searching for the answer.

"Who? Sanchez?" Ross offered. "He was easy. He was just offered a promotion to chief detective in Sacramento. He couldn't get out of here fast enough."

"What about Carla? Will she know I'm not dead?"

"It's handled. She's taken care of. Jim will fill you in on that." Ross gestured to the car. "Would you leave, please!"

"Call me in a couple of months," Alex said, hugging her forcefully. "You can get to meet Richard properly when we come visit." Margo looked at him, confused. He placed his hand at the side of his mouth and whispered, "He was the armed guard." He made a face like a schoolgirl with a secret.

"Get outa here now!" Ross said kissing her on the cheek. "Go!" He pushed Margo forward in the direction of the limousine.

Margo ducked her head lower and leaned into the car. She could feel Alex's helping hands on her backside giving her a gentle push. She hit the seat a little too fast and hard, and the blonde wig fell over her eyes. The car pulled away quickly, causing Margo to fall sideways. Someone grabbed her arm to help steady her, making her jump. She slid the wig back, enabling her vision.

"Well, I think that was an academy award performance, don't you?" Peta asked with a smile.

"Peta!" Margo screamed, throwing her arms around her friend. "What are you doing here?"

"Hey, someone has to teach you Portuguese," she said smiling broadly. "And as a true friend, I just can't let you drink your own coffee!"

Chapter Fifty-Six

Monique Washington ran her fingertip lovingly down the mane of the white ceramic horse in her hand. She replaced it carefully on the dresser next to a dozen others in various poses. She picked up a delicate silver frame containing a picture of a pretty white girl sitting atop a beautiful white horse on the beach. She ran to the window and compared the picture in her hand to the view outside.

"This was Cassi's room," Carla's voice said from the open doorway. "I wanted you to see her picture before we move her things out. Anything you want me to leave in here, I will. Her mom wanted you to keep whatever you like; we can remove. This is your room now."

"Can I keep the horses?" Monique asked meekly. "And this picture. Can I keep this picture?" She placed the frame down gently.

"Sure," Carla smiled. "I think Cassi would like that." Carla left Monique lying on the oversized four poster bed staring at the lace canopy above her, running her hands gently over the satin spread. She padded softly down the hallway and peered in the master suite down the hall. She saw the slender silhouette of Georgia Washington against the open French windows.

"Hi," she said quietly. "Enjoying the view?"

"Very much so," Georgia answered. "It definitely beats my old fire escape."

"Hey!" a voice shouted from the front hallway. "Where is this thing going?" The women walked out of the room quickly in response. Doug and Moses were carrying an old, beat-up easy chair toward the room. "This thing is heavy," Doug wheezed.

"Oh, my word!" Georgia exclaimed. "I didn't realize how bad that thing looked. I don't want it in here."

"What?" Moses gasped. "You said this chair went wherever you went."

"Well, that was before I saw this house," Georgia answered. "I can't put that ugly thing in here."

"Are you serious? We just lugged this thing down six flights of stairs!" Doug protested.

"Well, you can have it! Why don't you put it in the beach house," Georgia said generously.

"No. No. That's okay," Doug answered, with a little less than gracious expression on his face. "I have enough stuff of my own."

"Well, I don't want it!" Georgia stated sternly. "Don't bring it in here."

"What about the rest of it?" Moses asked sheepishly.

"I don't want it," Georgia said. "Give it to someone who needs it."

"Are you kidding me?" Doug asked exasperated.

"What? What's the matter?" Raul asked. He was standing awkwardly in the doorway, holding two large flowery vases.

"I don't want those either," Georgia declared. "You can take those to the shelter."

"To the shelter?" Moses mumbled. "We need to take those to the dump."

"I beg your pardon?" Georgia demanded.

"I said we're gonna take those to the shelter," Moses answered contritely. Georgia threw him a scornful look. A loud wail from the front door caught everyone's attention.

"Ohhhhhhh!" Melody moaned. She grabbed her stretched-to-capacity belly.

"What's the matter?" Raul asked.

"Ohhhhhhh!" She moaned again and looked down at her feet. Her legs were wet, and her sandaled feet stood in a good size puddle of water.

"Oh, my God! Oh, my God!" Raul began chanting. For whatever reason, he suddenly dropped both vases, and they shattered into pieces. "Oh, my God!" he continued.

"Well, that saved us a trip," Moses mumbled out of the side of his mouth.

"Raul!" Georgia shouted. "Stop that or I'm going to have to slap you." Raul obeyed immediately, and the annoying chant ended. "Carla, can I leave Monique here with you?" Carla nodded her assent. "Come on, honey," she said calmly to Melody. "We can take my car. I'll call you guys from the hospital." She ushered Melody gently out the front door.

"Here, Georgia," Carla called. "You might need these." She handed Georgia two large plush bath towels.

"I'm sorry," Melody said timidly, as they climbed into the car. "This is lousy timing. I guess I won't be house-sitting for you after all. I hope it doesn't mess up your plans."

"Oh, it won't," Georgia said. "Doug and Moses will be able to watch Monique. You just need to push that little one out tonight, so Carla and I can take some pictures with us tomorrow."

"I'll try," Melody smiled back.

"Good," Georgia replied. "'Cause I've got a wedding to go to."

Chapter Fifty-Seven

"By the power vested in me, I now pronounce you husband and wife."

Jim did not wait for the customary invitation to 'kiss the bride.' He scooped Margo into his arms as though she were a rag doll and kissed her fiercely. This was right, he knew. This had always been right, and he had always known it. What an idiot he had been. He finally released her, and they both emerged from the embrace, smiling broadly.

"This way! This way, Margo!" Peta's voice called excitedly. "Try and get a few of them with the priest," she directed the photographer.

Margo smiled in their direction obediently. She looked radiant dressed in a simple cream-colored lace sheath dress. A solitary white orchid with baby's breath adorned her up-do. She was barefoot, as was Jim, who wore a white linen shirt and Bermuda shorts. The perfect attire for a Brazilian beach wedding. One by one her friends approached her.

"Oh, my God! You look stunning!" Alex cooed. He kissed her affectionately on both cheeks. "Richard, Margo; Margo, Richard," he said with a flamboyant gesture of the hands.

"Hello, Richard," Margo said warmly, kissing him softly on the cheek. "And thank you," she said in memory of their last brief encounter.

"You're absolutely welcome," he countered. "Thank you for letting me be here today. I'm honored." His voice was deeper and huskier than she imagined it would be. He moved aside to let give someone else a turn at congratulating the bride.

"Oh, my God! Isn't he hot?" Alex said, rolling his eyes before padding along the sand after him.

"Congratulations, Honey!" Georgia said, kissing Margo. "I just told that man of yours that he'd better treat you right, or Carla and I will be flying down here."

"Oh, I think he will,' Margo chuckled. "But you can still fly down now and again to check." She hugged her friend closely. Georgia stood aside to let Carla move up front.

"Don't you dare!" Margo warned her, as the water welled up in her eyes.

"I can't help it!" she sobbed, as the tears escaped and rolled down her cheeks. "Cassi would be so happy to see this," she blubbered into Margo's ear. "I wish she were here."

"She is," Margo said breathlessly, touching the flower in her hair. Orchids were Cassi's favorite. "I can feel her." They held each other close in silence for over a minute before letting go.

"Okay!" Peta called. "Throw the, throw the bucket!"

"Bouquet!" Margo corrected. It was not often that an English translation eluded her companion. Margo kissed Jim lingeringly on the mouth, to a chorus of oohs and aahs from the small group, and then proceeded to walk a short distance up the beach. She stopped and looked coyly over her shoulder. "Okay, guys, here it comes." She hurled the flowers back over her head loftily. The ensemble scuffled.

"I got it! I got it!" Alex screamed, leaping high in the air, victoriously waving his trophy.

About the Author

Born and raised in Yorkshire, in the North of England. Entered into the gaming industry, and left the country in the mid-eighties to work in a Bahamas casino, where I met my future ex-husband, and moved to the US, in 1990.

As the mother of two young children, I became appalled with the stories of violence against women and children that were daily newspaper headlines, and flashed nightly on TV screens. These stories had such a sickening effect on me that I would imagine all the grisly things I could personally do to the perpetrators. I knew I could not possibly be alone in my thoughts. Other people had to feel the same way as I did. From that mindset came the idea to write a novel, hence, The Support Group was created.

Lightning Source UK Ltd.
Milton Keynes UK
UKOW041314031212

203110UK00002B/610/P